The Voyage

The Voyage

HUGH B. CAVE

Macmillan Publishing Company
New York
Collier Macmillan Publishers
London

First Edition
Printed in the United States of America
10 9 8 7 6 5 4 3 2 1
The text of this book is set in 12 point Baskerville.
Library of Congress Cataloging-in-Publication Data
Cave, Hugh B. (Hugh Barnett), date. The voyage. Summary: When his father escapes from jail and needs help hiding out, Vinnie feels he must choose between his parents. [1. Parent and child—Fiction. 2. Family problems—Fiction. 3. Cape Cod (Mass.)—Fiction] I. Title. PZ7.C29Vo 1988 [Fic] 87-24004
ISBN 0-02-717780-7

For Peggie, with love

The Voyage

O N E

When he got to the old tree, Vinnie Blake sat to rub the scratches on his legs. It was a hot July afternoon, and clawing around in the blackberry swamp had tired him. He took a handful of berries out of his pail and ate them one by one while catching his wind.

The tree at his back was a crazy kind of tree, split and bent years ago to show which way the trail went. Pa had never failed to stop and admire it when they came on it together. "You stand close to an Injun tree," Pa would say, "and if there's a breeze stirrin', you'll hear Injun voices off in the woods."

Vinnie had tried it but never heard voices, or anyway couldn't be sure they were voices. Still, the tree interested him. Studying it, he liked to think back on what the Cape Cod woods must have been like when only Indians lived here.

He was pretty sure things were different then— probably better than they were now. The Indians never went hungry long, for one thing. When they got stomach cramps from not eating, they just snuck up on a deer and *zing!*

Vinnie had stomach cramps right now. The blackberries didn't help, either.

He wondered if he had time to sneak a look at the camp. It must be four o'clock easy, because he'd been down in the swamp long enough to fill the five-quart pail. Ma would be peeved if he was not home to feed Rosanna her supper.

But Ma would be a little peeved anyway when she saw the rip in his pants. She'd tell him he was careless and didn't appreciate all she had to do with Pa gone. Ma was edgy lately.

He hid the pail by the tree, where none of the camp kids would be apt to come on it, and went down the sandy road at a slow trot, pretending he was an Indian and trying to step so his sneakers would make no sound. When he got to where the road curved into the camp clearing, he ducked into the woods.

The camp had been the site of a sawmill once, but the owners had sold it, lake and all, to some people up in Boston who had torn the mill down and put up tents and log buildings. The old sawdust pile was still standing, though. Vinnie crept to the side of it.

Today, for some reason, the camp was so quiet it seemed deserted. He studied the silent tents and buildings and the empty benches around the big central fire pit, and had a hard time biting back his disappointment. Watching the camp kids was about the only fun he'd had since Pa left.

They had everything, these kids. They wore fancy colored sweatshirts that said CAMP WILDEWAY on them, and they could go swimming or play games whenever they wanted to. Sometimes they ate their meals out-of-doors at long tables under a zinc roof, and, hey, the stuff they got to eat! It made Vinnie's stomach ache just to watch them.

2

He wasn't supposed to watch them. There were NO TRESPASSING signs all over the place. But it was fun, kind of. It was like getting in to see the movies in town. The town kids didn't have anything like this.

A man he recognized as the new camp director, Mr. Perkins, came out of a log building by the lake and walked as far as the fire pit. He was tall and skinny, with a thin streak of red hair on his lip, and wore tight khaki pants tucked into leather boots. He sat down and began to read a book, but looked up when a boy about Vinnie's age came out of a tent and called to him.

"Hi, Mr. Perkins," the boy said. "Can you hear them yet?"

Mr. Perkins tipped his head sideways as if he were listening. "No, but they ought to be in soon," he said. "How's your leg, Steve? Feel better, does it?"

The boy looked down at his right leg and Vinnie saw it was bandaged. He was a red-haired boy with a million freckles. "It still itches. I could have gone, though."

Mr. Perkins said, "It's better you didn't, I think," and began reading again. Then he put the book down and checked the watch on his wrist. Frowning, he looked across camp toward the low, zinc-roofed building that Vinnie knew was the camp kitchen. He said to Steve, "Is the cook back yet?"

"I haven't seen him, Mr. Perkins."

Mr. Perkins looked annoyed but only sat there. Steve went past toward the lakeshore, limping because the bandage held his knee stiff.

From the sawdust pile, Vinnie squinted at the camp kitchen and pondered the meaning of what he had heard. The cook was away, and there might be no one in the kitchen. There seemed to be no one at all in camp except Mr. Perkins and Steve.

He flattened out and wriggled along in back of the pile to the row of tents. He was not merely pretending to be an Indian now. His stealth was real.

At the rear of the kitchen he rose. Mr. Perkins was still over by the fire pit. Steve had limped out to the end of the pier where the rowboats were tied. Vinnie opened the kitchen door and ducked inside. He knew where the food was kept. Many a time he'd hid in the woods and looked through that door, watching the cook at work.

He opened the refrigerator and began grabbing. There wasn't time to be choosy. If it was good to eat he wanted it because food was almost always a problem now, with Pa gone. After stuffing his pockets and the front of his shirt, he closed the refrigerator and turned to sneak out again.

Right then the front door opened and Mr. Perkins stepped in. He couldn't have suspected anything; it just happened. Seeing Vinnie, he stopped short in pure surprise before letting out a yell that froze all the muscles in Vinnie's legs.

"You, there! What do you think you're doing?"

Vinnie stood hoe-handle stiff, his eyes swelling till they felt like horse chestnuts. When he got his wits back, it was too late. Mr. Perkins grabbed at him and he fell sprawling. Before he could even scramble away on hands and knees, the camp director grabbed again and had him.

At that moment the red-haired boy named Steve appeared in the doorway. "What's the matter?" he asked, advancing slowly upon Mr. Perkins and Vinnie. "What'd he do, Mr. Perkins?"

Mr. Perkins made a show of removing the stolen objects from Vinnie's pockets and shirt. "This boy is a thief, Stephen. I think you had better let me handle him."

Steve came no closer than the end of the long kitchen table and stood there watching.

"What's more," Mr. Perkins said, "this undoubtedly explains the other missing items." He fixed Vinnie with a threatening gaze. "You've been here before, haven't you?"

"I never! I never took anything else!"

"Who are you? What's your name?"

Vinnie looked away, trying desperately to think. "What is your name?" Mr. Perkins repeated.

"M-Manuel."

"Manuel what?"

"Correra." It was a made-up name, but Mr. Perkins just might believe it.

"How old are you?"

"Ten."

"Where do you live?"

"I ain't tellin'! But I never stole before! Anyone that says I did is a liar!"

Mr. Perkins looked uncomfortable. He was not a hard man, Vinnie guessed; what he seemed like was a kind of weak man with a lot of troubles on his mind. He stood there for a minute, undecided. Then Steve came a step closer and said, "What are you going to do, Mr. Perkins?"

"I . . . ah . . . I . . ."

"He only took things to eat," Steve pointed out. "Maybe he's hungry."

"Please, Stephen," Mr. Perkins said.

Vinnie could read him now. Mr. Perkins was a man scared of appearing weak. If Steve were not here, he would most likely have delivered a lecture on stealing and then said, "All right, Manuel Correra, you can go now if you promise never to come near this camp again." But with Steve watching him he didn't dare. Steve would tell the other kids and Mr. Perkins would be laughed at.

"Stealing is a serious offense," Mr. Perkins said. "I'll have to think about this." He took a firmer grip on Vinnie's wrist. "You come with me."

The boy with the freckles and bandaged leg stepped back against the wall, staring, as Vinnie was led past him to the door.

Vinnie would have twisted free and raced for the safety of the woods if he could. He was no longer frightened. The first shock had passed and he felt only anger. For Pete's sake, he'd only wanted a little food to take home, and they had tons of it in that kitchen. He could have told Ma that Liz Maple gave it to him. Liz owned a grocery store in town and often did give him things.

His thoughts were interrupted by a shout, and Mr.

Perkins stopped. A boy came running over the top of the sawdust pile, waving his arms. Others followed, and in a minute the place was full of kids all talking at once in loud voices. They swarmed around Mr. Perkins and for a time, in their excitement, didn't seem aware of Vinnie.

"I won it, Mr. Perkins!" one yelled.

"I'd have won it if I hadn't got mixed up at the crossroads!"

"Hey, Mr. Perkins, that number six clue was mean!"

Mr. Perkins smiled and nodded and tried to answer all of them at once. At last he held up a hand for silence. "There will be another treasure hunt next week," he announced. "Now run along and get cleaned up for supper." He seemed anxious to get them away before they noticed anything was wrong. But by then they were aware of Vinnie and one of them said, "Who's this?"

Mr. Perkins looked like a man who felt his troubles would never end. Patiently he explained that Vinnie—only, of course, he called him Manuel Correra—had been caught stealing. This caused the camp kids to crowd closer, to see for themselves what a thief looked like. They were rich kids, mostly, who wouldn't know about such things. They wouldn't know how it felt to be hungry, either.

Vinnie stood the staring as long as he could. Then he muttered savagely, "Aw, go chase yerselves!"

Looking shocked, Mr. Perkins hustled him to the cabin.

It was a small cabin with only one window, and Vinnie saw right away that he would not be able to get out of it. The door was fitted with a padlock, and the screen at the window was held in place by fastenings on the outside. The screen was of tough wire, too, not plastic.

The cabin contained a cot and two chairs, one of them a soft armchair, and a bookcase and a desk. On the desk was a neat white cardboard sign that said, in black letters, MR. PERKINS.

"You are to stay here until I have time to talk to you," Mr. Perkins said while locking the desk drawer and putting the key in his pocket. "And I warn you, don't make any more trouble."

He turned away. But as he was about to close the cabin door on his way out, a boy wearing a bright red sweatshirt came toward him from a group at the fire pit. The boy carried a pail.

"Mr. Perkins," he said. "Look."

Mr. Perkins paused in the doorway. "Yes, James?"

"Look at what we found up the road, by that old Indian tree." The boy set the pail down. "You know, the tree where the number nine clue was hidden? A whole pailful of blackberries!"

Mr. Perkins looked at the pail. "You have no idea who picked these?"

"There wasn't anyone around, Mr. Perkins."

"I see. But, of course, they do belong to someone. We can't—"

"They're mine!" Vinnie said fiercely. "I picked 'em!"

Mr. Perkins turned to frown at him. "You picked them?"

"I can prove it! That's my pail!"

"Just where did you pick them?"

"Down in the swamp." Vinnie almost bit his tongue when he realized what he'd said. The swamp was camp property. But it wasn't really a swamp—that was only what the local kids called it—so maybe Mr. Perkins wouldn't know what he meant.

Mr. Perkins did, though. He smiled a tight little smile, as if he were getting hold of an idea that pleased him. Then he said, "What you call 'the swamp,' young man, is part of this camp. You were trespassing!"

"Nobody ever picks those berries! They'd rot!"

"But there are signs." Mr. Perkins turned his back on Vinnie to motion the other boy away from the door. "Take the pail to the refuse hole, James, and dispose of it. I think we may have found an excellent solution to our problem."

Vinnie looked at him wide-eyed, unbelieving. "You mean I can't have my pail back?"

"I mean you may not have your pail back. Yes. Precisely."

"But that's stealin'!"

"Just as you were stealing, young man. First the blackberries, then food from our kitchen. And I still say you've stolen other things, so you can stay right here until I return." And Mr. Perkins walked out, locking the door behind him.

Inside the cabin Vinnie talked to himself in a low,

choked-up voice. Thinking of what Ma would say when she found out he'd been locked up and had lost the pail, he wanted to snatch the MR. PERKINS sign from the desk and hurl it to the floor and stamp on it. Then his flood of rage flowed into a deeper, darker channel and he sat rigid in the easy chair, gripping its arms fiercely with both hands, ready to fight for his freedom if given a chance.

He had been sitting there only a few minutes when a sound at the window made him turn his head. At the screen was the face that belonged to the red-haired boy with the bandaged leg, Steve. Afraid to accept the boy's sign of friendship, Vinnie only glared at him.

"Hey!" Steve whispered. "Hey, Manuel!"

"Whatcha want?"

"Come here, will you? Luvva Pete, I can't yell it!"

Vinnie hung back. It might be a trick. Any time a strange kid got friendly, watch out. But Steve kept motioning to him, and at last, slowly and warily, Vinnie approached the window.

"Perkins is over in the kitchen," Steve said quickly. "You want me to get you out?" His face, all freckles, was close against the screen, denting it. His hands already struggled with the fastenings.

Unexpectedly the screen came loose and fell with a shivering sound to the ground.

"Come on!" Steve urged. "Hurry up, will you?"

Vinnie needed no more than that. He grabbed the sill and pulled himself up, easy for a kid who could claw around for wild blackberries all day. Wriggling through the opening, he twisted himself like a cat and landed on his feet at Steve's side. Instantly he looked around, half expecting Mr. Perkins to be standing there, waiting to seize him again.

But it was no trick. From the rear of the cabin to the safety of the woods was only a few steps, and the cabin would hide him most of the way from the kids at the fire pit. He peered into Steve's face, bewildered because the camp kid had done this for him.

"Won't you get in trouble, lettin' me loose?"

"Not me. Perkins'll think you got the screen open yourself."

"He'd have to be dumb to think that."

"He's dumb, all right, and mean. He's not our real camp director—just filling in because the real one is sick."

"He sure talks," Vinnie said.

"Yeah. He jumped on you because a lot of stuff has been disappearing lately—canoe paddles, baseball gear, last week two brand-new hammocks—and he knows he'll be held responsible. Did you take any of that?"

"No."

"I knew you didn't. It's the cook doing it. Everybody knows, but Perkins is just dumb. Look, what's your real name?" Steve grinned. "You can tell me," he said. "It isn't Manuel Correra; I know that. You wouldn't be crazy enough to tell Perkins your real name."

Vinnie drew back, ready to fight if the boy laid a hand on him. This might be it, the catch in turning him loose. "That's my real name," he said, and added quickly, "I have to go. I can't stay here talkin'!"

"Wait. Here." The freckled boy thrust out his hand. In it lay a crumpled five-dollar bill. Vinnie scowled at it, bewildered.

"Go on, take it," Steve insisted. "I've got more. My dad's a judge, and I get an allowance. Here, take this, too." He scooped out the contents of a pants pocket and pressed a fistful of change on Vinnie, as well. "Take it. You can buy some food with it!"

Vinnie took it and ran. Fear put wings on his torn sneakers. He had a horror of anything that came easy. Steve's money might be some part of a scheme cooked up by Mr. Perkins to get him in deeper trouble. He didn't think it was, but it could be.

His feet flew over the sand and carried him to the safety of the woods before he dared to look back. Steve was walking toward the pond, whistling, as if nothing had happened. Mr. Perkins stood in the kitchen doorway, peering at the watch on his wrist.

Still scared and puzzled, Vinnie ducked into the woods and lit out for home, slowing to a walk only when he was winded. He was way past the old Indian tree when he stopped to count the money Steve had given him. It came to five dollars and sixty-seven cents and a bronze medal.

The medal wasn't worth anything, he guessed. Probably Steve hadn't meant to give it to him. It was pretty, though. On one side were an Indian head—a chief's head, with feathers—and the words CAMP

WILDEWAY. The other side said FIRST AWARD, LEAD-
ERSHIP, STEPHEN DENNIS.

Vinnie studied the name, Stephen Dennis. As he
buttoned the medal up in his back pocket for safe-
keeping, he wished he'd told Steve his right name.

T W O

*F*or a week there had been no rain. The
road was dead dry, and a cloud of dust
rose in Vinnie's wake as he crossed the field to the
house. Even the house looked dusty. It was no big
deal of a house, he had to admit, but that was
because Pa had built it with no help and not much
money. Never mind. Pa was a first-class carpenter.
Everyone in town said so.

About eight feet from the back door he paused to
listen. If Rosanna was crying, it would be his fault
for being late.

He heard instead a sound of singing. Ma was singing in the kitchen and the song was a French song,
loud and quick, with lots of la-la-la-ing. Ma had
come to Cape Cod from a place called Quebec, in
Canada. At any rate, she had come to the city of New
Bedford from Quebec, and Pa had brought her the
rest of the way after falling in love with her and
making her his wife. He'd been in New Bedford

working on an old whaling ship that was to be fixed up for some kind of museum. Pa was good with boats.

The song Ma was singing was loud, and she didn't notice him even after he shut the door behind him. The door opened straight into the kitchen. Ma stood with her back to him, turning the handle of a meat chopper with her right hand while her left scooped up chunks of cooked meat from a plate and fed them into the machine. The song went with the handle-turning.

She was singing, Vinnie saw, to Rosanna, who was in her high chair on the other side of the table. Rosanna didn't know French any more than he did. She didn't know more than a few words of English. So Ma was probably singing just for a joke. That must be it: a joke.

She stopped to get a breath, or because the song was done, and Vinnie laughed. Quick as a flash of lightning she turned to face him.

He'd been wrong. It wasn't any joke. Somehow he was almost always wrong lately when he dared to guess what Ma was thinking. By the glitter in her eyes he knew she was mad now.

"Where've you been?" Her voice reached like a broom into all the corners of the room and swept out the lightness and the la-la-la-ing, leaving only an emptiness.

But Vinnie was not scared. He knew her too well. Ma would not take her hand to him just for being late.

"You know where I've been," he said. "After black-berries. I told you where I was goin'."

Ma frowned as though remembering against her will. "Well, where are they?"

"What?"

"The berries. You brought some home, I hope."

Vinnie moved sideways to a chair at the table and sat, not shifting his gaze from her face. You had to be wary lately when talking to Ma. Her moods could change quick as a wink. "I sold 'em," he said.

"Sold them? Who to, for heaven's sake?"

"Mr. Perkins, at the camp. Now, don't go lightin' into me. I never went near his old camp. I met him on the road and he asked would I sell the pail of berries for five dollars, and I sold 'em. Here." Vinnie fished the five-dollar bill out of his pocket and held it out to her. He didn't offer the change the red-haired boy had given him, though. Or the medal.

Ma didn't take the bill right away. She looked at it, scowling with her whole face, then peered at Vinnie sideways. "Are you tellin' me the truth, young man?"

"I'm givin' you the money, ain't I? The whole five dollars!"

"What would Mr. Perkins want with a pail of black-berries?"

"Well, he could use 'em at the camp, couldn't he? Those camp kids wouldn't go down in the swamp after 'em!"

Ma shook her head. Vinnie guessed she didn't wholly believe him. But she snatched the bill from his hand and jammed it into a pocket in her dress, because the money sure would come in handy. What Pa had left them when he went away was almost gone now, and Ma got only a few dollars for a batch of bayberry candles. Making candles was slow work, too. It kept her busy at night long after Rosanna was put to bed.

The money softened her some, even if she didn't believe the lie. "Wash up and you can feed your sister," she said. "Go on, now. Get some hot water off the stove and scrub those hands good."

Vinnie went around the heavy oak table to the stove and carried the kettle to the sink, pausing to take hold of Rosanna's foot and shake it as he passed the high chair. Rosanna's giggle pursued him, and at the sink he turned to grin at her. She was a cute kid, not even two years old yet. She never cried, either, or almost never. With just an old bent spoon to play with, she'd laugh at herself or try to talk, and if nobody paid any attention to her, that was all right; she didn't care.

He scrubbed his hands and dried them, and by that time Ma had Rosanna's supper ready. She pushed it across the table to him: a bowl of warm cereal with milk, and a cup of warm milk to go with it.

Vinnie pulled a chair up to the high chair. "Know your name?" he said. "It's Rosanna. Say it. *Ro-zanna.*"

Rosanna clapped her hands and said it, and he swung about with a whoop of delight. "Hear her, Ma? She can say it every time now!"

"She's learning," Ma said. But her black eyes shone. He knew she was pleased.

"Say *sup-per*, Rosanna."

Rosanna said it.

"Ma! Didja hear that?"

"You get some supper into her," Ma said, "or you'll be hearing things out of her you don't want to." But she wasn't peeved. That was just her way of talking. Vinnie guessed she was even pleased about the five dollars. A new pail at Liz Maple's store wouldn't cost that much, he was sure, and that old dented one should have been thrown out long ago. He grinned again at Rosanna as he fed her.

He was fond of Rosanna. He'd liked her from the very first day, when Pa arrived home from the hospital, in the old pickup he'd owned then, and said, "You got a baby sister, boy. Come on, let's celebrate." If he lived to be a hundred, he would never forget that day.

The two of them, he and Pa, had gotten into the pickup and gone to a place near Sagamore, on the canal, where there was a carnival. Pa had some extra money; he'd been reroofing a summer place that belonged to a man from New York. They bought ice cream cones and hot dogs. They rode on the Ferris wheel, with Vinnie scared he'd get dizzy and fall, and Pa yelling just as loud for the sheer joy of it. They threw baseballs at milk bottles and tossed wooden rings at things on a platform inside a fence. If you got a ring over the thing you wanted, you won it.

Vinnie had wanted a swell big harmonica that glittered like it was made of pure silver and gold. He tossed rings at it till his arm ached, without any luck because they bounced so much, and then Pa tried, and finally Pa said to the man, "You win, friend. It's too much for us. But my boy here wants that confounded thing and he's got to have it. Yes, sir, today he can have anything in the world he takes a fancy to."

The man shook his head. "You mean you want to buy it? Nothing doing."

"Friend," Pa said, "today my wife brought a baby girl into this fair world—the cutest little button of a girl you ever laid eyes on. We're celebrating, and I want that harmonica for my son. You name your price."

"Well," the man said, getting friendly, "that harmonica cost me close to six dollars."

"I'll give you twelve."

"You give me six," the man said, "and we'll call it even." He took the harmonica off the platform and handed it to Vinnie, and then, glancing at Pa and seeing the pleasure in Pa's face, he suddenly grinned and said, "No, by God, I won't sell it. Keep your money. This is on me."

"For nothing?" Pa was astonished.

"For nothing."

"Oh, boy, thanks!" Vinnie said. "Thanks a million, mister!"

"Don't mention it," the man said, laughing as if he had just found he felt good.

That was the queer thing about Pa. He did things sometimes that made Ma worry, but most people truly liked him. Everywhere he went, people talked to him and seemed to feel better for it. Maybe it was because Pa liked people. But look out if they made fun of the way he talked sometimes. He wouldn't stand for that.

"A man has a right to dream," Pa had said once, explaining to Ma how he'd gotten into an argument with someone. "Anyone who makes fun of him for that is just plain ignorant. If nobody ever dreamed, mankind would still be living in caves." Vinnie would never forget the way he'd said that, standing in the middle of the kitchen with his eyes blazing.

After leaving the carnival the day Rosanna was born, they'd driven around some before heading for home. Sometimes Pa would drive fast, with the old truck pounding along like a cement mixer, and sometimes he would just mope along singing songs. He knew a million songs, Pa did. Mostly they were sea songs.

Then on the way back he'd turned the car down a side road that led to the ocean. He and Vinnie got out and walked over the dunes to a deserted little beach Pa knew about, and went swimming.

It was late when they got home. Pa got out the crib he'd made for the new baby and said it wasn't good enough. He was probably the best carpenter in a hundred miles, but he said the crib wasn't good enough! He knocked it apart and rebuilt it, while Vinnie sat on the floor beside him, handing him the tools when he needed them. Pa never once said, "It's past your bedtime." He worked right on till after midnight and then said, "There! What do you think of it now, boy?"

"It's swell, Pa."

"No," Pa said, "it isn't swell. To be good enough for a little girl born in the image of your mother, it would have to be made of solid gold and studded with diamonds. But we did the best we could." He stepped back to look the crib over, and nodded. "Your mother wants to call the baby Rosanna, Vinnie. Like that, do you?"

"Sure."

"So do I. And I'm going to paint it on the end of the crib here."

He did, too. Vinnie didn't see it done because he fell asleep watching and Pa must have lifted him up and put him to bed. But in the morning the name was on the crib in fancy letters. Pa had clearly worked hard on it.

No, Vinnie would never forget that day. Thoughts of it filled his mind now as he spooned cereal into Rosanna. The memories made him feel good, but they saddened him, too. He wondered where Pa was, and what he was doing. And if he ever remembered. Because Pa had been gone six months or more, and it seemed like forever.

THREE

Ma kept watching him.

Vinnie didn't mind at first. She often sat and looked at him, and then after a while she would say he ought to have a new pair of shoes, or his clothes were getting so worn she was ashamed of him. He knew then she only stared at him to help her think.

Tonight, though, he didn't want her to think about him too hard. He would have to tell her the truth about what happened, of course—she was death on lying—but first he had to plan how to do it.

"Vinnie," she said at last.

"Yeah?"

"Where'd you meet Mr. Perkins?"

"Well, I . . ." He could see it was no use. He could think up a likely story, sure, but the bigger the lie the more he'd get bogged down in it. Taking in a big breath, he looked straight at Ma and blurted out the truth.

For the longest time she didn't say or do anything. Then she sat down and said, "Were you really that hungry, Vinnie? Enough to steal?"

"Well, I thought I was. You, too, Ma. I mean, we haven't had much to eat lately."

"I know." Ma looked kind of sad. "And Mr. Perkins took your pail of berries to punish you?"

"Yeah. But Steve Dennis must have figured it wasn't fair, so he gave me the money to make up for it."

"You shouldn't have lied to me, Vinnie."

"I'd have told you, Ma. Honest."

"Yes, I believe you would have. All right. I'll think about it." Ma stood up and turned back to the stove. "You go ahead and feed your sister."

He spooned the last of the cereal into Rosanna and lifted her out of her high chair. She was sopping wet. After carrying her into the bedroom, he laid her on Ma's bed and put a dry diaper on her, then held her just over the mattress in the crib Pa had made and dropped her so she bounced a little. She laughed and clambered onto her feet for him to do it again.

She was pretty, Rosanna was. Pretty like Ma. She had the same white skin Ma had. Vinnie wondered about that at times, because he looked more like Pa. He was like Pa in other ways, too: always wanting to be near the ocean, for instance. Always wanting to go where you could smell the sea and look at boats.

Once he had asked Ma about it, right out, and she had said, "You do take after your father." Then she'd added, "I hope if you grow up to be a carpenter, you're as good a one as he is. But if you neglect your responsibilities, being good at anything won't help you much. Do me a favor and remember that, please."

When he'd held Rosanna up and dropped her a few times, Vinnie said sternly, "That's all now, you go to sleep," and spread a blanket over her, jamming it under the crib mattress so she couldn't work it loose. Then he went into the other room and sat down to his own supper, ground-up meat that had been warmed in gravy and poured over a piece of bread. Ma filled a glass of milk for him and sat down and watched him eat. After a while she said, "I see you tore your pants again."

"I fell in the swamp. I can fix it."

"I'll mend it," she said. "You don't have to be so big and independent."

"Well . . ."

"Never mind, now. I've got something to tell you."

Vinnie stopped eating and looked at her.

"I met Clayton Sawtelle in the village this afternoon," Ma said quietly, "and I asked him if he could give you a job. He said he can use you three days a week at the boat shed till school begins. You're to start tomorrow."

Vinnie put the fork back on his plate, and his mind filled up with a picture that scared him a little. Everybody knew old man Sawtelle. He built boats, but people said he was years behind the times doing it. Building boats was all he ever thought about, too, they said.

"Mr. Sawtelle is a fine man," Ma said, as if she could read his thoughts.

"What will I have to do?"

"Lord, I don't know. Whatever he tells you to, I suppose. I never worked for him."

"Ma, do I have to do it?"

"Yes, you have to do it. It won't hurt you, either, doing a little work now and then."

"It's work pickin' blackberries and goin' after bayberries for the candles, ain't it?"

"I mean real work, and don't say 'ain't.' It might be you'll actually learn something for a change."

"It sure won't be any fun workin' for that old bastard."

Ma got up and took a step toward him. "Don't use that word!" she said angrily, and stood over him with her hand raised, ready to take some kind of action if he talked back.

23

Vinnie didn't answer her. He sat still, pushing hard against the back of his chair but staring straight up at her, meeting the glitter of her black eyes. He ran his tongue along his lips and waited, knowing better than to move or speak until her anger went off the boil. When he couldn't stand her looking at him any longer, he took up his fork again and forced himself to eat. He couldn't taste what he was eating, but he finished it.

Ma swept the empty plate and glass from in front of him and carried them to the sink. "Get your water in," she said.

"All right."

"I won't have language like that in this house. Not where there's a baby learning to talk."

"I never meant nothin'."

"Very well. I believe you. Go on now, get your water."

Vinnie picked up the empty pail by the stove and went out the back door with it, fighting his tears. She didn't have to rip into him for every little thing, did she? It wouldn't be any fun working for old man Sawtelle, if what people said about him was true. What would a kid like Steve Dennis say if someone told *him* he had to work for Sawtelle?

It was not dark yet, but the woods at the edge of the field were filling with shadows, and the telephone poles along the road stood out sharp against the evening sky. His feet set up a rustling in the dry grass as he plodded through it, letting the night air cool his feelings. Pa and he had sometimes gone for long walks in the evening, he remembered.

The well was in back of the house near the edge of the field: an old one with a roof of weathered boards over it and a rusty iron crank for lowering and lifting the bucket. He paused two or three times before he got to it. Once a catbird streaked up in front of him with a rush of noise, like a startled partridge. Once he stopped to look back at the house for a minute.

Let her wait for the water. Someday when she talked to him like that, he'd just clear out and never come back. She'd be sorry then, with only her and Rosanna left, and no one to haul water or cut wood or hunt bayberries for her candles.

At the well he set his pail down and lowered the wooden bucket. It thumped against the stones and hit with a muffled splash, and for a while he just stood there, not ready to crank it up again. Then all at once he heard a sound that caused him to jerk his head up and look toward the nearby woods.

Only one person in the world could whistle like that, lifting a soft, liquid note way up high and holding it so it fluttered like a moth's wing at a window-pane!

With a quick look at the house to be sure Ma was not watching him from the doorway, Vinnie circled the well and ran. It was almost night-dark there at the edge of the woods. He couldn't see anyone. But he knew where the whistler ought to be standing—right there where the path broke out of a black-alder thicket into the field. He pulled up, breathless, and before he could look around or call out, a calm voice spoke to him.

"Hello, youngster."

Pa hadn't changed much in the months he'd been gone. His soft, dark eyes that never took on a glitter the way Ma's eyes sometimes did were the same. Vinnie stood and blinked at him and said at last, "Pa! I never knew you were back!"

Pa laughed a little and squatted down to rest on his heels. Maybe the months he'd been away had seemed a long time to him, too. He studied Vinnie's face and put a hand out to feel his arm.

"You've got a birthday coming soon, hey? You'll be eleven."

"Uh-huh."

"You don't stack up very solid for that old. You gettin' enough to eat?"

But Vinnie didn't want to talk about things like eating. Not now. Not when he had to get back to the house before Ma suspected something and came looking for him. Pa might be going away again. This might be the only time they'd have together!

There were a million questions he wanted to ask, and he grabbed at Pa's arms. "Are you comin' to the house, Pa? Did you have to go away? Can you stay with us now? Can you, Pa?"

"Whoa," Pa said. "One at a time."

"But I have to get back with the water! Ma will come after me."

"I won't keep you. You just listen for one minute; then you can go."

"I'm listenin', Pa! I am!"

"All right, boy. Now, I don't know what your ma

26

told you, but I've been in jail. And I'm not supposed to be out just yet, see? Some really rough characters were breaking out and made me go along with them. I'd overheard their plans, see, and they didn't want me talking. Lord, I only had a little more time to serve, but I had to do it."

Pa paused for breath. "Now what happens I don't know. If your ma wanted me back, I'd just give myself up and get that jail term over with. But she says she doesn't want me, and I can't see myself going back to jail for nothing. Anyway, I know a real smart place to hide while I think about it, and if you're careful about being watched, you can come there and we'll talk. That's why I came back here, Vinnie—to see you and find out how your ma and Rosanna are."

Pa smiled, running his fingers through Vinnie's hair, and his smile showed the white teeth Ma always said were the best and whitest on Cape Cod. "You know that old wreck in the cove near Dunner Point?"

Vinnie bobbed his head up and down. "I went out to it once."

"I'll hide in that," Pa said. "I'll go there and make me a hiding place in that old schooner. Be snug as a beetle in a floor crack. Soon as you get a chance, you come and see me. But don't you tell a living soul I'm back. Not your ma yet, or anyone. You understand?"

Vinnie bobbed his head again.

"All right, boy." Pa caught Vinnie in his arms and squeezed him, chuckling as if it were all a tremendous joke they were going to play on people. "Scoot now. Tell your ma you fished a sea serpent out of the well and had to shinny up a tree when it chased you." Laughing his soft, whispery laugh, he gave Vinnie a little push toward the house.

Ma was folding diapers at the kitchen table, but turned her head as Vinnie let the door slam behind him. "It took you long enough," she said.

Vinnie set the pail down beside the sink. He knew what she would say if he told her a sea serpent had treed him. "I saw a shootin' star and wished on it."

"Wished for what?"

"I can't tell, can I? If you tell, it doesn't work out."

Ma stopped what she was doing and gave him a queer look. "You're a funny one. Wherever'd you hear that?"

"I dunno. I guess I just heard it. Maybe from Mary Raymond."

"Well," Ma said, "I'm not sure it's right. I've kept my wishes to myself, Lord knows, and they haven't worked out too well." She drew up a chair and sat down. "You never knew I wished for things sometimes, did you?"

"I dunno what you mean."

"No, I guess you don't. You're just a boy. Maybe I ought to remember that more often. Vinnie . . ." She put a hand out and motioned him to come closer, and when he did she began to trace a design on his shirt with the tip of her finger. She did that to help herself talk. "Vinnie," she said, "I don't mean to be at you all the time. Honest. It's just that I get so scared sometimes."

Vinnie looked down at her finger, not knowing what to say.

"I get scared you'll turn out to be too much like your pa," she said. "Lord knows, you've got all his good points." She raised her head, and her eyes were dark and shining, not bright like glass but shining softly like pond water at night. "Your pa *has* his good points," she said. "I forget that sometimes, I suppose. He loves you and Rosanna. He loves me, too, I guess. But . . . but . . ."

Whatever Ma wanted to say, it was clearly too much for her. It rose up inside her and gagged her. She gave her head a shake and stood up.

"All right," she said. "Take your wish to bed, whatever it is. Be careful you don't wake Rosanna."

Vinnie went into his bedroom. It was off the kitchen, like the one Ma shared with Rosanna, but it was smaller. His bed was a cot pushed up against a wall that had a window in it.

Sitting on the cot in the dark, with the door open just a crack to let some light in from the kitchen, he took off his clothes and rubbed the scratches on his legs. Then he put on his pajamas and went to close the door.

"G'night, Ma."

She was folding the last of the diapers. "Right after breakfast you go and see Mr. Sawtelle," she told him. "Remember, now."

"All right."

"And Vinnie . . ."

"Yes, Ma?"

"I'm sorry I got mean. I guess I . . ." She came around the table and sat on her heels in front of him, acting as if she were afraid he might run away. All of a sudden she put her arms around him and squeezed him up against her, burying her face in his pajama jacket. For maybe half a minute she held him that way without saying a word. He could feel her trembling.

"Vinnie," she said then, "don't get the idea I'm always down on you. I'm not. Honest. You don't think I am, do you?"

"I guess I had it coming," he said.

"You're a good boy most of the time." She let him go. "Sometimes I forget."

"It doesn't matter."

"I'll remember from now on," she said. "I'll try real hard to remember."

Vinnie shut the door and slid under the covers. He didn't feel like going to sleep. When Ma acted like that, it scared him; he didn't know what to make of her. Tonight it was worse because he had just talked to Pa.

A tingle of excitement raced through him at the thought of Pa's being so close to home. He sat up in bed and leaned on the windowsill, peering out at the woods.

Pa was back! He hadn't gone away to get free of them, as Ma had hinted at; he'd been in jail—and not for something real bad, either, or he wouldn't have had only a little more time to serve. Now he was home again, for a while, anyway. The thought ran through Vinnie's mind like one of Pa's crazy songs, sending a wave of joy clear to the soles of his feet.

F O U R

*F*rom the windows of the boat shed Vinnie could see the Atlantic Ocean, stretching clear away to what must be a whole different world somewhere. It was blue-black, what he could see of it, and it washed a sandy shore below a bluff on which the Sawtelles, father and son, lived and built their boats.

If you could believe what people said, old Clayton Sawtelle had been master of many a ship on that ocean, small ships and big ones. He was retired from all that now, though, and only in his face could you see signs of what he used to be.

Wesley Sawtelle, Clayton's son, was different. Wesley was old, too, of course—he must be close to forty, Vinnie figured—but he was not dried up yet. He was the kind of man Ma would call handsome, meaning he had good wide shoulders and a pretty face and smooth pink skin. He grinned a lot when old Clayton was not watching him.

Wesley had been alone in the shed when Vinnie arrived. There was an upturned box in a corner, screened from the doorway by an unpainted skiff resting on sawhorses, and Vinnie had walked around the skiff and discovered Wesley sitting there.

He was on the box with his legs stretched out and his back against a bench and a dreamy look on his face. It was the kind of look Pa used to have sometimes.

When Vinnie coughed to catch his attention, he looked up and grinned. "So it's you," he said. "Come on in."

Vinnie was late. He had left the house right after breakfast, but instead of making straight for the boat shed he had cut across the highway half a mile below and ducked through the woods to the cove. He'd had to see if Pa was aboard the old schooner yet.

He hadn't seen anything, though. Just the old hulk resting there same as always on the sandbar where a storm had driven her six or seven years ago. On the beach were some skiffs left by men who went out after hard-shelled clams called quahaugs, but there was no sign of any boat tied up to the schooner. Of course, Pa might have swum out. If the police were after him, it wouldn't be safe for him to row out and tie a boat up where it could be seen. Vinnie just didn't know. But when it got dark tonight he would find out.

He braced himself and looked at Wesley. "I know I'm late. You can take it out of what you pay me."

The younger Sawtelle leaned forward to study him, then nodded. "Now, that's the spirit, Vinnie."

"I never worked at buildin' boats before. You'll have to tell me what to do, I guess."

"Do?" Wesley said. "Why, sit down."

Puzzled, Vinnie looked for something to sit on, found a sawhorse handy, and did as he'd been told.

"The next thing you do is keep an ear cocked,"

Wesley instructed. "When you hear the old man approaching, jump up quick as a fiddler crab and pretend you're busy. Not that he's a slave driver, mind you. He just can't stand seeing anyone idle."

"Pretend I'm busy at what?"

"Why, anything, more or less. If I were you I'd just grab that old broom there and begin sweeping."

Finding the man's talk beyond his understanding, Vinnie looked with interest at the unpainted skiff. Living on Swamp Pond Road was good for some things, like you got to know the trails through the scrub pine and gray birch and where "mushrats" built their houses along the shores of little dark-water ponds; but you hardly ever set foot in a salt-water boat.

He went over to the skiff and studied it, admiring the way each curved board was snug up against the next one, giving the boat its shape. The sanded wood smelled like checkerberry leaves.

"Will I get to work on boats like this?" he asked, lifting his head to look at Wesley.

"That's what we're making at the moment," Wesley said.

"Hey, neat!"

"Uh-huh," Wesley said. "That's the kind of thing the Sawtelles manufacture just now: monarchs of the bounding main, in the fine old tradition. Why, one of these days that sleek vessel you're gazing at may be tossing the sea from her teeth in a dash around Cape Horn, or flashing her fine white sails under a tropic sun."

Puzzled, Vinnie looked at him. It was strange

hearing Wesley talk that way. That was how Pa talked sometimes.

"That is," Wesley went on with a grin, "if she isn't tied up in Dunner Cove with a rake and a bucket of quahaugs in her." He stood up, stretching his arms above his head. "Well, shall we get to work? The last boy we had here began his noble career by cleaning up the place. You might as well do the same."

Vinnie sent a last look at the unpainted boat before reaching for the broom. That comment about white sails under a tropic sun stuck in his mind, and he wished Wesley had not made fun of it. Pa always talked about far-off places as if he were in church talking to God, though he'd never been to any faraway places that Vinnie knew about. The difference was, Pa's kind of talk made you feel good and Wesley's didn't.

When Clayton Sawtelle came into the shed later, Vinnie was stirring up a cloud of dust. The old man eyed him and nodded, making a grunting sound when Vinnie paused to look at him. That was his only greeting. His seamy face tightened into an expression half scowl and half squint as he walked over to peer at the unfinished skiff. Then he went to a corner of the shed and began sorting some cans of paint laid out on the floor.

Vinnie went on sweeping. Wesley glanced at the old man and said, "Well, aren't you going to hello the boy?"

"I said hello."

"Well, then, can't you tell him what to do?"

"He's doing it."

"And when he's finished?"

It seemed Clayton would stand for only so much. He swung about with a glitter in those cold blue eyes. "We'll have an understanding here and now about this boy," he said, speaking slowly in a voice that was almost too quiet. "I hired him, and I'll undertake to make him useful. If he doesn't work out, I'll admit my mistake. Is that clear?"

There was a moment of silence while Wesley returned his father's steady gaze, and Vinnie watched both of them. It was Wesley who at last shrugged and looked away. The old man moved his craggy head in a half circle, peered at Vinnie without any expression, and then with another grunt returned to his paint cans.

It was a trying morning for Vinnie. He swept the shed floor and carried the sweepings to a pit outside. He stacked lumber. He cleaned paintbrushes, pressing them soft in a can filled with something Clayton mixed up, then rinsing them in a bucket of soapy water. He was busy and glad to be busy, yet after each small task he had to wait until the old man thought of something else for him to do.

At noon, with half an hour to himself—not enough time to visit the cove to look for Pa—he took the bag of sandwiches Ma had fixed for him and went to the edge of the bluff. Sitting there in deep dry grass, with his legs dangling over a sod ledge high above the beach, he gazed down at the blue-black water and felt miserable. It was pure torment being penned up here when the cove was so close.

The two peanut-butter sandwiches finished, he pushed himself over the edge of the bluff and went sliding down the gullied red-sand slope to the beach. A mess of stones skidded down after him, boiling about his feet when he stood up.

He looked back. The shed and house were hidden by the cliff's overhang. The beach was empty and wild-looking, the surf feeling its way in through black boulders crusty with mussels. The air was cool and light.

He walked to the water's edge and stood there thinking about Pa. It was funny about Pa. All his life he'd probably never been more than a few miles from the Cape, yet he was always talking about places like the South Seas and the frozen north and the jungles of Africa. He was all for going to those places someday, Pa was. When he spoke of them his eyes lit up and you could tell he was there already in his mind.

And what about Clayton Sawtelle? He'd actually been to some of those far-off places and knew what they were like. But you'd never guess it to hear him talk. Clayton seemed a good deal like Ma, Vinnie decided—all for a no-nonsense kind of life.

The afternoon was no improvement over the morning, but toward the close of it something happened. Clayton had given the upturned skiff a coat of white primer. When that job was done and Vinnie had been handed the brush to clean, the old man pulled a wooden box from under a workbench and dumped a set of stencils out of it. They were all mixed up, letters and numbers scrambled together and some of them stuck with paint.

Pawing through them, Clayton seemed to get more and more exasperated as he picked out those he wanted and laid them to one side. It took him a long time. Finally he slapped a handful of letters down in front of Wesley and said, "We'll be needing these soon, I expect, and, as you can see, they were put away dirty. Show the boy how to clean them."

Wesley motioned Vinnie to him. "I trust you got the point," he said. "*I* put them away dirty. Truth is, we won't be needing a name on that boat for days yet, but he knew these were in this condition and he's been itching to confront me with the fact, like a man with money in the bank just aching to spend it. Anyway, take a putty knife and get the paint off them. Here, like this." He spoke without lowering his voice, wanting Clayton to hear him, then picked up one of the thin metal letters and worked on it awhile. "Think you can do it?"

Vinnie nodded.

Wesley turned to his father. "He'll get them ready for you. I have to go to Provincetown."

"What for?" the old man asked with a frown.

"To see a friend."

"A girlfriend, I suppose you mean."

Wesley shrugged. "Is there something wrong with that? I'm not quite as old as you are, you know."

Maybe Clayton didn't like being told he was old, or maybe he didn't approve of Wesley's doing anything but work. Whatever it was, he jabbed his hands against his hips and stood there stiff as a gnarled old scrub pine, glaring, as Wesley went past him to the door. Then for a long time afterward, as he moved about the shed, he kept snatching things up and slamming them down again, as if his feelings had spread through him like tree roots in a waste pipe, reaching even to the ends of his fingers.

It was four-thirty when Wesley left, and after five before Vinnie finished scraping the paint off the stencils. Vinnie didn't know what to do then. He thought it must be time for him to go home but was afraid to suggest it. Pretending to be still busy with the putty knife and sandpaper, he toyed with the letters, moving them about, arranging and rearranging them on the bench. He supposed they spelled the name of the skiff, and tried to discover what it was.

Clayton said suddenly, "Do you know how to fit those together?"

Vinnie shook his head.

"Here." The old man snatched up a *W* and an *I* and joined them, his blunt fingers teasing them into place. "Put them together and go home. They spell *Wildeway*"—he wrote the word on a piece of paper— "for that camp over on Wedge Pond."

Vinnie looked down at the stencils and was numb with fright. He picked up one of the letters as if it were a hot coal and dropped it. When he tried to speak, he stuttered. "Is this b-b-boat for Mr. P-P-Perkins?"

"It is. Why?"

"I didn't think—I thought it was for quahauging. Will Mr. Perkins be comin' here?"

"I expect so," Clayton said slowly, and repeated with a squint, "Why?"

But Vinnie had been in tight situations before and managed to wriggle out of them, frightened or not. "Why . . . I didn't think a man like Mr. Perkins would want a real good boat like the ones you make, Mr. Sawtelle. I'd have guessed he'd want something made out of plywood or fiberglass or some other dumb stuff." And knowing it was a good answer, he turned from the curious stare of Clayton's blue eyes and went to work on the stencils again. But the fear inside him flowed like ice water.

For a moment he continued to feel the force of Clayton's steady gaze on him. Then without further talk the old man turned to the paint cans.

Vinnie grooved the letters together, wet his lips, and stepped back from the bench. "I got it done. Can I go now?"

Clayton walked to the bench to be sure the job was done to his liking. He took out his watch and looked at it. "You can go."

"When will I come again?"

"Day after tomorrow, I suppose. I promised your ma I'd use you three days a week."

"Mr. Sawtelle . . ."

Clayton only grunted, scowling down at him.

"If you'd rather I didn't come back, I won't. Only I wish you'd tell Ma. She'd be real down on me if she thought I dogged it on purpose to get fired."

"You don't need to talk like that," Clayton said, looking angry.

"Well, I just had a notion—"

"I said you don't need to talk that way." Clayton reached out to lay a gnarled hand on Vinnie's shoulder. "I told your mother I'd give you some work, and I'm doing it. You be here Wednesday." Then, fishing a roll of money from his pocket, he separated a ten-dollar bill and slapped it on the bench alongside the stencils that spelled *Wildeway*. And with a grunt of farewell he walked out, leaving Vinnie standing there.

F I V E

It was too late for Vinnie to go home by way of the cove. If he wasn't in time for supper, Ma might suspect something. When he walked into the house, Rosanna was in her high chair and Ma was feeding her.

"Mr. Sawtelle kept me late," he said before she could scold him. "I ran most of the way."

Ma surprised him by saying, "You must be tired. It was a long day, I bet."

"I can feed Rosanna."

"You don't have to. Sit and rest."

Ma finished with Rosanna and said Vinnie could put her to bed if he liked, so when he had washed his hands he lifted her from her high chair and carried her into the bedroom. She said "sup-per" and "Ma-ma" for him, and because in his mind he was already racing out of the house on his way to the cove, he almost said "Pa-pa" to see if she would repeat it. He caught himself just in time.

At supper Ma asked what he had done at the boat shed, and he told her. She seemed proud that he had a real job now. She asked all sorts of questions: what kind of boats he worked on, how he got along with Clayton and Wesley, what they said to him. She seemed to know that Clayton was not easy to work for because she made Vinnie repeat all he could remember of what the old man had said and done.

"He and Wesley don't get along too good," Vinnie told her.

"Why do you say that?"

"Wesley quit early and went off to Provincetown to see some lady friend. Mr. Sawtelle didn't like it."

"I expect it was the quitting early he didn't like," Ma said. "He's pretty strict on discipline, I hear."

"What's discipline?"

"You work for him, you have to toe the line." Ma didn't say it as if she disapproved; she spoke as if she were pointing out something good about the old man. "Anyway," she said, "I'm glad you're getting along with both of them. I knew you could if you wanted to." Then she let Vinnie finish his supper in silence, and he was able to think about the scheme he had worked out for getting away from the house.

He could get away all right; he was sure of that. When Ma was in a good mood you could do almost anything with her. Funny thing about Ma, she almost always wanted to be happy. Give her a chance, and she'd get over one of her moody spells so fast it left you blinking. She was real pleased with him this evening. She'd let him out all right.

"Ma."

She looked at him, ready to smile. "What, Vinnie?"

"Can I go over to Mary Raymond's awhile and play with the new dog she got?" Mary Raymond was a girl his own age, and they were good friends. He didn't have many friends, but Mary and he stuck together in school and visited back and forth pretty often.

Ma didn't answer.

"I been workin' hard all day, Ma. Honest I have. I won't be home late."

"Well, I guess so. Long as you're not late. Get some water in first, though."

Vinnie grabbed the pail and was out the back door like a scared deer, racing for the well. He was half-way back when he heard a car coming up the road.

The machine stopped in front of the house and he stopped, too, setting his pail down because it was heavy and he suddenly knew there was no use hurrying anymore. It was a state police car, and two men wearing uniforms got out of it. They were looking toward the house.

Vinnie stood where he was, trying hard to think what he ought to do. If he left the pail on the back steps and scooted across the yard into the woods, they maybe wouldn't see him. Ma would tell them, if they asked, that he'd gone to the Raymonds'. He could hurry down to the cove and tell Pa.

But if they were looking for Pa, Pa would want to know what they said and did, wouldn't he? It wouldn't be any help to him just to know they had come to the house.

Vinnie hated to do it. He was almost certain Ma would not let him out again after the police went. But for Pa's sake he had to. He went on in, and as he set the pail down he said, "There's a car out front. A police car." And then one of the men knocked on the front door.

"Oh, my Lord," Ma said. Yanking her apron off, she tossed it at Vinnie and told him to hang it up, and on the way to the door she tugged at her dress and fussed with her hair. Before opening the door she took in a big breath and sort of shook herself all over, as if to shake her clothes and body into place. Vinnie backed up to his bedroom doorway.

The two men stepped inside. Vinnie didn't know them and he guessed Ma didn't either, because one of them asked Ma if she was Mrs. Joseph Blake, and she nodded. He said he was Lieutenant Hill and the other man was Sergeant Freitas and they would like to talk to her. Lieutenant Hill was a big, square man. The sergeant, taller but younger, frowned at Ma and Vinnie, then only looked on while the lieutenant talked.

"I won't keep you long, Mrs. Blake," the lieutenant

said. "Your husband got away night before last, and it's natural for a man to head for home after escaping from jail."

Ma put a hand against the edge of the table, and for a few seconds her face was blank. Then she began to tremble, as if the thought of Pa's coming back had touched a secret hope deep inside her and sent a kind of electric shock through her. The color ran out of her face, leaving it almost dead white.

All of that happened before she spoke. When she did speak, she was not pleasure-shocked or scared anymore, only angry.

"He wouldn't dare come back here," she said in a low voice.

Lieutenant Hill said, "Does he know you feel this way?"

"Well, I told him. I told him there'd be no starting over this time."

"He wouldn't have any hope of a reconciliation? I mean, he isn't a hardened criminal, Mrs. Blake. All he did was get into a fight with some fellow who called him 'Jesus Joe' or something. And he didn't really break out of jail, ma'am. I mean, we know he was forced to."

While waiting for Ma to answer, the lieutenant looked at Sergeant Freitas, and the sergeant nodded to show he agreed.

Ma thought about it awhile and then shook her head. "No," she said. "We won't be starting over. I hate to say it, but that's the way it has to be." She spoke the words slowly, and Vinnie supposed she meant them. At the same time he remembered the way she'd begun to tremble only a few minutes ago, and wondered if she had to make herself mean them.

"I see," the lieutenant said.

"We've got our lives pretty much in order now," Ma said. "I even went to see Joe in jail and told him not to try to come back."

The lieutenant wrote something in a notebook, then tore the page out and laid it on the table. "If you find out he's in the neighborhood, Mrs. Blake, we'd appreciate a call," he said. "Do you have a phone?"

"No, but there's one at the Raymonds'."

"You can call this number." He looked at Vinnie and seemed about to add something, but didn't. Then Sergeant Freitas opened the door and both men said good-night. Ma stayed in the doorway, staring after them until the car was gone.

Ma was silent for a long time after the men left. She walked around the room, sat down, got up and walked again, all the time looking as if she were about to say something but not saying it. She kept glancing at Vinnie, and Vinnie stood in his bedroom doorway wondering if she would let him out.

She sat down at last with a heavy sigh and said, "I never told you your father was in jail. I didn't want you to know."

Vinnie looked at her.

"Only a few people did know," she went on, rubbing a finger on the table as if she were writing something. "It happened when he was working on a house in Fall River. You've never been there. They didn't bring him back here, just came and got me and I went there to see him."

Vinnie kept on looking at her.

Ma stood up. Her mouth was trembling and there was a queer twist to her face when she halted in front of him. Vinnie guessed she was about to say something she didn't want to.

"There are some things you need to think about," she said. "I guess you know your pa was a fine man when he settled down and worked hard. He's a real good carpenter; everyone says so. But he's a dreamer, too, and never seemed to keep a steady job long enough for us to get ahead. You know that. I don't have to be telling you."

Vinnie nodded.

"He talked big," Ma said. "Oh, yes, he talked big. And sometimes we actually did have a little money in the bank, like when he went away. But I never knew what to expect from him. You remember that. Don't you ever forget it."

She was quiet for a few seconds. Then she went on, "In some ways you're a lot like him, Vinnie. That's why I get scared sometimes. On the other hand . . ." Shaking her head, she stepped back. "Well, never mind. Maybe you inherited only the good side of him, if that isn't too much to pray for. But remember what I said. If your pa comes sneakin' back here, I don't want any trouble. He's caused us heartaches enough."

She stopped to run her tongue over her lips. "No matter how we feel about some things," she finished, "that's how it's to be. You hear?"

No matter how we feel. That was what she had said: *No matter how we feel*—meaning she still had some good thoughts about Pa. Vinnie suddenly had good thoughts about *her*. But all he did was nod.

"Did you bring in the water?"

"It's there by the sink."

"Well, all right, then. Just remember what I said." She turned away, wiping her hands on her dress.

Vinnie waited a few seconds, then said, "Can I go down to Mary's now, like you said?"

"Yes, go along," Ma told him. "Right now I'd as soon you would."

He ducked around her and ran, clawing the door shut behind him.

S I X

The moon was pale behind racing clouds when Vinnie slid down the cliff to the lonely strip of beach by the cove. Far down the shore, lights shone in the windows of quahaugers' houses. The old schooner, two hundred yards out, was only a dark smudge that looked more like a rock than a ship.

No one ever fooled around the cove at night, he knew that. Only the quahaugers bothered much with it in the daytime. But he stayed quiet in the shelter of the cliff, trying to see in the dark and hear through the sharp sighing of the wind, until he was certain the shore was deserted. Then, like a fiddler crab in full flight, he made straight for the nearest boat.

He turned the skiff over and found a pair of oars under it, as he'd expected. By using one for a lever, he was able to work the craft into the water. Climbing in, he sat down to row.

He was lucky the weather was good, he told himself. Getting out to the old schooner would be easy tonight. In a wind, when the sea rolled in past Dunner Point with the whole Atlantic behind it, the cove was no place for a boy in a rowboat.

He rowed with short, jerky strokes, turning his head every now and then to line up with the schooner. The moon stayed half hidden. The water was black and mean looking, and cold as winter. He was glad when the schooner suddenly loomed up alongside and from its deck Pa's voice reached down to him.

"Vinnie?"

"It's me. It's me, Pa!"

"Row around to the other side, to the hole."

Vinnie had been out to the old schooner only once in all the years she'd been here, and had forgotten about the hole in the side of her that faced the sea. He nosed the skiff into the opening and Pa reached down and caught it. "Grab my hands," Pa said, and lifted him onto the deck.

That schooner was a strange place for a man to be hiding, Vinnie thought. The owners had long ago removed her engine and everything else of value, and she was just an empty shell. Water sloshed around inside her, filling her with noises. Now, as Pa led him down into the cabin, warning him to watch out for a broken step, he felt scared.

But his jittery feeling didn't last long. With the door closed, Pa struck a match and lit a lantern hanging on the bulkhead, and then Vinnie looked around in amazement.

There were two beds in the cabin, though he guessed maybe they weren't called that. One was covered with a moldy old brown blanket. Tucked away in little cubbyholes forward were a sink and a stove. In the middle of the cabin was a table, and beside that a nail keg that Pa was using for a seat. Everything was old, but still it was like a dream.

"Oh, boy!" Vinnie whispered.

Pa said with a soft chuckle, "Make yourself at home. Sit down on the bed there."

Vinnie sat, still looking around. Then, though he hated having to do it, he said, "Pa, the state police are lookin' for you."

When Pa spoke after a few seconds of silence, his voice was slow and heavy. "You mean they came to the house?"

Vinnie told him about Lieutenant Hill and Sergeant Freitas and the questions they had asked. When it came to repeating what Ma had told them, his voice faltered. "She said she wouldn't help you if you came around. Maybe she only said it to throw them off, but I don't think so. I think she meant it."

"She meant it," Pa said.

"Well, *I'll* help you. You can count on that!"

Scowling, Pa rubbed the black stubble on his face. "I'm not sure you should have come here," he said.

"It may have been a foolish thing to do."

"I had to tell you, didn't I?"

"Well, yes. But they might have followed you." Pa blew out the lantern and made for the steps, calling back over his shoulder, "You stay down here till I look around."

Vinnie wriggled back on the bed and sat there without moving, feeling miserable to think he might have done something to help the police find Pa. If they found him, they'd put him back in jail, wouldn't they? Back in jail! He could hear Pa on deck, on the side of the ship that faced the beach. The passing minutes seemed like hours.

Then the cabin door opened and closed again, a match sputtered, the lantern painted the walls yellow, and he saw that Pa's face had lost its tightness.

"I guess we're all right," Pa said. "I don't see anyone ashore. You want to be careful, though. They could have followed you without half trying."

"I'm sorry, Pa. I never thought—"

"Forget it. Tell me about your ma and Rosanna."

Relieved, Vinnie leaned back against the bulkhead and talked, but after a while the schooner began to enfold him in its spell again and he hardly knew what he was saying. On his other visit to the ship he hadn't explored the cabin; he'd been afraid the schooner might suddenly fill up with water and turn over with him inside her. He had never seen the inside of any ship this big before.

"You know something, Pa?" he said when Pa stopped asking questions about home. "It's just like a house in here. Better'n a house, even!"

"You're right," Pa said. "And if this old boat was fixed up, a person could go clear around the world in her."

"Around the world, Pa?"

"That's what I'd like to do," Pa said proudly. "If not clear around the world, then certainly to some far-off places. I've been giving it a lot of thought, Vinnie. Seems to me I don't have much choice anymore. There's no point in going back to jail if your ma doesn't want to make a fresh start when I get out. So all that's left for me is to fix this old boat up and make a new life for myself."

"Hey," Vinnie whispered. With the water sloshing around in the old schooner, filling her with sea sounds, he almost had the feeling he and Pa were sailing away in her right now.

"By the way," Pa said, "where are you supposed to be tonight?"

Vinnie was lost in the sea sounds. "Huh?"

"Where did you tell your ma you were going?"

"Oh. To Mary Raymond's."

"Was that wise? Suppose she says something to Mrs. Raymond and finds out you didn't show up there."

"She won't say nothin'. Ma and Mrs. Raymond are kind of on the outs right now."

"Those two are on the outs? Why?"

"Well, Ma said somethin' about you bein' just a dreamer, and Mrs. Raymond said she shouldn't run you down that way. It'll blow over quick enough, but right now I'm pretty safe."

Pa shook his head. "You know, there most likely

isn't a better woman on the face of this earth than your ma. But she's too good for her own good. She can't stand to see anyone with an honest failing."

Vinnie was silent.

"What makes it worse," Pa said, "is that she thinks a lot of things are failings when they're not. You, now, you're more like me. What you said a few minutes ago proves it."

"What I said?"

"You said, 'I bet we could go clear around the world in this old boat!' Or did I say that? Never mind, we both thought it." Pa sat there grinning, but looking small and thin inside his baggy old suit. "You've got the right slant on things, Vinnie," he said. "Your ma, now—if she was to walk into this cabin, she wouldn't see any fine ship flying before the wind. She'd only see that the blanket there beside you is dirty and the bulkheads ought to be painted."

"Well," Vinnie said, "I guess I'd want to clean her up, too, before I went anywhere in her."

"Of course you would. That's not the point. Your first thought was big."

Vinnie liked the sound of that. "And you'll be goin' around the world now, Pa? You mean it?"

"It's one of the things I've always hoped to do."

"Boy!"

"This is a big world," Pa said, looking thoughtful there under the lantern, "and I'm not content with the little I've seen of it. When I shut my eyes, I think of typhoons in the China Sea and icebergs off the

Horn. I see a white-sailed schooner lying under the cliffs of an island in the Marquesas. I see—well, never mind. The point is, I've read books, boy. I've read about men who do things. I want to do some of those things, too."

Vinnie sat on the bed with his hands clasped about his drawn-up knees and looked at Pa and listened. He got a pleasant, tingly feeling when Pa talked that way—kind of like the feeling he used to get when Pa was cutting his hair and the comb stroked his neck and the click of the scissors made him drowsy. Ma cut his hair now and he didn't get that feeling so much. He wished he didn't have to go home for a while. At home, if he so much as tracked a smudge of dirt onto the floor, he was told to clean it up. Here he had his feet planted square on the bed Pa slept in, and Pa never so much as noticed.

The truth was, he wished he could go away with Pa to the places Pa was talking about. And maybe he would, when the time came. Right now he had to head for home before Ma began to wonder what was up. Ma wouldn't go down the road to the Raymonds' after him—she wouldn't leave Rosanna alone in the house for even a second—but if she suspected anything, there'd be trouble.

"Pa, I got to go."

"I guess you'd better," Pa said. "When do you suppose you can come again?"

"Tomorrow night, if Ma lets me out."

"I need food," Pa said. "I can get water for myself—there's a spring at the foot of the Point—

but food's a problem. All I had to eat today was a lobster I got out of a pot. Can you get me something to eat, do you think?"

"I'll try."

"I expect I'll lie low here and fix this old boat up. By the time she's ready, the hunt for me will have died down and I can sail her out of here. But I'll need food, and there's no way I can get any unless you bring it."

"What should I bring, Pa?"

"Try to get food I don't have to cook," Pa said. "There's this old stove here—I cooked the lobster on it—but I can't be walking all over creation for firewood. Someone might notice the smoke, too." Then, "Hey!" Pa said, looking as if he'd all at once got hold of a great idea. "What about Liz Maple?"

"What about her?"

"Well, she and I have been good friends for years. You know that. Of course, she might not want to get involved in helping a man the police are looking for, but the worst she can do is say no. Go see Liz, why don't you? Tell her I'm here on this old boat and I need help. See what she says."

"All right," Vinnie agreed. He, too, was fond of Liz Maple. Whenever Ma sent him to buy things at her store in the village, Liz found time to talk to him, asking him how he was and how things were going at home. "By the way, Pa," he said, "where'd you get those clothes you're wearin'? They're not yours."

"No, they're not mine. One of the fellers I escaped with said it was a shame, making me go with them when I had only a couple of months left to serve. So we went to where a cousin of his lived, and the cousin gave me these out of the goodness of his heart."

Vinnie had just thought of something. "Pa," he said, "that lieutenant, the one who came to the house, said you were in jail for fighting. I didn't know they put people in jail just for that. Is fighting all you did? Huh?"

"Well, I guess I hurt the man. I didn't mean to, but . . . No, that isn't true. I meant to hurt him, all right, but not so much. Hurting him that much was an accident." Pa shook his head and heaved a sigh. "But never mind that. You go see Liz. You hear?"

"I will, Pa. The first chance I get."

"And be careful. Don't you breathe a word to anyone but her." Pa put out the light and opened the door. "Hang onto me now," he warned. "Watch this broken step."

At the hole in the schooner's side, Vinnie dropped down into his borrowed skiff. The moon was out from behind the clouds now, and he saw a second boat alongside his own, an old one with broken thwarts. One of its oarlocks was fastened together with wire.

"Is this how you get back and forth?"

"I took it from a summer rental place that nobody's living in," Pa said. "Found the lantern there, too, and the matches I'm using. The boat's no good; the owner probably won't even report it missing. I didn't dare take one from the cove here, and besides, it wouldn't have been right. Those quahaugers work hard for a living."

Vinnie nodded. He was friends with a quahauger kid in school, and from what the boy said, it was no easy work his father did, standing in a boat for hours on end with a heavy, long-handled rake or tongs, harvesting those hard-shelled clams off the sea floor.

"Why didn't you hide out in the empty house instead of here, Pa?"

"Because an empty house is the first place the police would think of. And because I told you I'd be here, and I had to make sure you'd find me." Pa reached down and gave Vinnie's shoulder a squeeze. "You be careful with this quahauger boat when you put it back, boy. Be sure to leave it the way you found it. I'll see you tomorrow night."

"G'bye," Vinnie said softly.

But Pa didn't hear, or didn't feel like answering. The only sound was the slapping of the sea against the side of the schooner.

S E V E N

*I*n the morning, after feeding Rosanna her breakfast and eating his own, Vinnie asked if he could go to the village.

"What for?" Ma said.

"To the library."

"What do you want at the library?"

"To see if they have any books about boats, Ma. I ought to know more about boats if I'm gonna work for Mr. Sawtelle."

Ma gave him a sharp look as if she thought he might be lying, but his face must have fooled her. She shrugged and said, "Well, all right, I guess. But don't you be gone the whole day."

"I won't, Ma."

It was a nice morning and he didn't mind the two-mile walk to the village. He even passed up his usual shortcuts and went the full distance by road, so as to stop and talk to Mary Raymond. She was out in her yard.

"Hi!" she said. "Where are you headed so early?"

Vinnie stood at her fence and watched her come toward him, her yellow hair looking as if the sun was rising in it. She was far and away the prettiest girl in the school he went to, and it was really special, having her for a friend. He told her he had to go to the village, so he couldn't stay and talk. But she was glad he had stopped, anyway. He could tell.

He hurried then, suddenly realizing that if he couldn't persuade Liz Maple to help Pa, he would have to think of some other way to get food. That would take time. Of course, he couldn't go to Dunner Cove till dark, anyway, or someone might see him, but time was precious all the same. As he walked along, the sun warmed him and there was a nice clean smell from the pines along the road's edge, even though the weeds and grass under them were gray with dust.

In the village he cut through the playground behind the red-brick town hall, then crossed over to the drugstore and went down the hill past the Palace. A new space picture was playing there, he saw by the posters out front. He wished he could see it, but not today.

Next to the theater, down the hill, was Maple's grocery. Beyond the entrance to the grocery was an old green door. Vinnie looked in the store window to see who was waiting on customers, and it wasn't Liz, it was her helper, Bill Clay, so he went on to the green door and opened it and climbed a flight of worn wooden stairs.

At the top was another green door. He knocked on that, and a voice boomed out, "Yes? Who is it?"

"Me. Vinnie Blake."

The door opened and a big woman wrapped in an old blue robe stood there, smiling down at him.

"Hello, Liz," he said.

Liz stooped to peer into his face. She smelled of lilacs. "Vinnie," she said, "I haven't seen you in days. Where've you been?"

"Oh, around."

"You shouldn't stay away so long. Liz worries. You know that, don't you? Come on in."

He walked in and sat in an overstuffed green chair that was getting pretty old and worn. The ends of its arms felt as if glue had hardened on them. It was a comfortable chair, though, and it was his, kind of, because he'd been using it ever since his first visit here, a long time ago. He still remembered that.

The visit he remembered best, though, was one he had made after Pa went away. It was a Saturday. Rosanna was sick and Ma couldn't leave the house, so she sent him to Liz's store for some things she needed for supper. And while he was fishing the money out of his pocket to pay Liz, she started talking to him. She asked him how Ma was, and Rosanna, and then she said, "Are you in a hurry, Vinnie?"

"No, ma'am," he told her, "so long as I get back with this stuff in time for Ma to fix supper."

"Well, I'm just about to quit here and go upstairs to my place for some cookies and milk," Liz said. "I don't suppose you would turn down cookies and milk, would you?"

"No, ma'am."

Liz had talked to him a long time that day, here in this front room of her apartment above the store. What she wanted, he knew now, was to find out if he and Ma and Rosanna were getting along all right with Pa gone away. He didn't know Pa was in jail then, of course. If Liz knew, she wasn't about to tell him, either. She gave him a ham and some cans of food to take home, and told him to explain to Ma that she was fixing the store over and didn't want to throw things out. "And if you come back next week, I'll have other things for you," she said.

The following Saturday he'd called on Liz again, but not to take any food. "Ma says we don't need anything we can't pay for," he had to tell her, using Ma's exact words because she'd made him learn them before he left home.

"You ate what I gave you, I hope," Liz said.

"Yes, ma'am. But I can't take any more."

"You look hungry right now," she said. "I bet you walked here on an empty stomach."

"No, I didn't. I had breakfast."

"Just what did you have for breakfast?"

"Well, some oatmeal. I had some oatmeal."

"Ha!" Liz said. "And you a growing boy. I made some beef stew this morning for my lunch. More than I could eat in a week. Have some."

He was scared to take anything from her after the way Ma had acted, and, anyway, he wasn't real hungry. Ma said she had to be careful with the money they had, that was all. "I had some kind of stew yesterday," he said. "Honest."

"Not like mine, you didn't," Liz insisted. Then, laughing, she pulled him into the kitchen and made him sit down at the table there. The table was covered with oilcloth that had little dark red roses on it.

Since then he'd eaten with Liz pretty often. When he went to the village alone he usually called on her, and she almost always found time to give him something. The queer thing was, she never asked any questions. Oh, she might ask about Ma and Rosanna, how they were, but never more than that. She never mentioned Pa at all, even though the whole village knew she and Pa had been friends before he married Ma. You couldn't go steady here without the whole town knowing about it.

Anyway, he liked her. And not just because she gave him things to eat, either. He liked the way she talked. She talked the way Pa did sometimes, about places she would like to go to. Not the same kind of places, maybe. Not the South Seas and around Cape Horn and like that. Mostly it was big cities Liz wanted to go to. But she made it sound exciting.

He sat in the old green chair now and looked at her. "Liz, can I ask you something?"

"Of course you can."

"You remember when you wanted me to take some food home and I couldn't?"

"Yes, I remember."

"Do you still have some?"

"For you to take home, you mean?" Liz looked surprised and then kind of puzzled. "Why? Is your ma short of food?"

He shook his head. "It wouldn't be for us. It's for Pa."

Liz looked at him as if he'd told her something that made no sense. "Are you talking about *your* pa? About Joe Blake?" she said.

"Yes, ma'am. He's back."

"Back where? Where is he?"

"If I tell you, will you promise not to tell anyone?"

"If he doesn't want me to tell anyone, of course I won't," Liz said. "I'm probably the best friend your pa ever had or will have. Where is he?"

Vinnie told her. "And he hopes you can help him out, Liz. He needs stuff to eat that doesn't have to be cooked. If you have any you want to give him, I can carry it home now and hide it near the house somewhere, and take it to him tonight."

"Hide it? You mean your ma doesn't know about this?"

"No, ma'am. She told the police she wouldn't help him if he came around."

"So he's hiding in that old schooner and relying on

you to find food for him. Is that it?"

Vinnie nodded. "And I can get it to him without Ma knowin' about it, either by sayin' I'm goin' over to Mary Raymond's or on my way to work."

Liz's face took on a puzzled look again. "Work? What work, for heaven's sake?"

Vinnie told her about the job he had at the boat yard. When she seemed pleased about that, he leaned toward her and said in a pleading voice, "Have you, Liz? Have you got any stuff I could take to Pa, so he won't have to go away?"

"Of course I have," she said.

He was so glad he almost let out a yell.

"What do you suppose he'd like?" Liz asked.

Vinnie thought about it. "Maybe some corned beef?"

"Corned beef. All right. What else?"

"Condensed milk? That wouldn't spoil, would it?" He began to feel frantic, knowing there must be all kinds of things that didn't have to be cooked if only he could think of them. Why hadn't Pa told him what to get?

"How about sardines?" Liz said. "They keep all right."

"Yeah. Sardines."

"Some vegetables, too, don't you think?"

"Uh-huh." It was going better now, and he bobbed his head up and down. "In cans, huh?"

"Fresh would be better. But, of course, if he doesn't have a stove . . ."

"There's an old stove on board," Vinnie said, "but

he'd have to hunt high and low for wood. People might see the smoke, too."

"All right, then. I get the idea." Liz pushed herself up out of her chair and went to the door. "You wait here. I'll see what I can find in the store."

"Can't I come with you?"

She shook her head. "No, you better not. If folks see you goin' out of my store with a box of groceries, they might ask questions. You don't usually buy much."

She was right, Vinnie guessed. Besides, it wouldn't be long before the whole town knew about Pa getting out of jail and that the police were looking for him. They might remember seeing Vinnie Blake with groceries and guess whom he was taking them to.

Liz shut the door behind her and he heard her going down the stairs. Getting up, he went to a window, one that was propped open with a stick, and stood there watching people go up and down the street.

It was a pretty nice town. He wished Pa liked it better and didn't always talk about places a million miles away.

He thought about Liz, how in the beginning he had called her Miz Maple and she'd stopped him. "You call me Liz, you hear?"

"Yes, ma'am."

"Liz. L-i-z, Liz!"

"Liz," he said, grinning.

"That's more like it." Suddenly she'd wrapped her big, warm arms around him and squeezed him up against her. "I like you," she said. "You come in and talk to me whenever you want to, you hear? I'm all alone, and I like to talk to people. If I take to them, that is."

She was a wonderful person. He just wished Ma and she were friends, but probably they couldn't be, with Liz being the woman Pa gave up to marry Ma.

He heard footsteps on the stairs again, and Liz came back in, out of breath from climbing. She didn't have any box of groceries, and for a second Vinnie thought he had failed. He was truly scared. But after dropping onto a chair and getting her breath, she looked at him and nodded.

"Go out the back way," she said. "You'll find a box by the rear door of the store, in the lane. I hope it won't be too heavy for you."

Vinnie thanked her.

"You won't find everything in it that we talked about," Liz said, "or it would have been too heavy. You'll be coming again, anyway. This can't be a one-time thing."

Vinnie nodded.

"Tell your pa I'm praying everything will turn out all right for him," Liz said. "Remember now. And you're a good boy, Vinnie, to be helping him this way. I'm proud of you."

E I G H T

Vinnie went out through the kitchen and down the back stairs into the lane. The groceries were where Liz had said they would be, in a cardboard carton tied with rope.

The box wasn't heavy. By the time he was out of town with it through back streets and open lots, though, he was ready to rest awhile. Then, resting, he wondered what he ought to do about the library. If he didn't have at least one book when he got home, Ma was sure to be suspicious and ask questions.

He couldn't face that. Sure as fate he'd get rattled and say something that would give the whole thing away—Liz, and Pa being on the schooner, everything. Getting up, he looked for a place to hide the box of groceries and finally found a bull brier thicket that looked mean enough to be safe. His hands were a mess of scratches by the time he got the box into it, but that was all right.

He'd been gone a long time, he guessed. Worried, he ran all the way back to the library and up the steps.

Mrs. Chase, at the desk, said, "Well, are we here for something special, or do we just like to be out of breath?" She was a middle-aged woman with a thin, red face who talked that way at times, but the kids liked her.

He stood in front of the desk and told her he was working at Sawtelle's boat yard now and would like some books on boat building if she had any.

"Well, yes, we do," she said, "though they may be a little outdated, I'm afraid. But that won't matter if you're working with Mr. Sawtelle, will it? I mean, everyone says he builds boats the old-fashioned way. And who knows but what it's the best way, too."

She must have known just where to look, because she was back in nothing flat with two books. "There," she said, slapping them down on the desk. "You glance at those and see if they'll help you."

Right away he saw that they would, because they were full of drawings and pictures of small boats like the Wildeway skiff he had worked on. He made himself look through them slowly, though, not wanting to seem impolite or in a hurry, and after a while Mrs. Chase said, "So you're working at Sawtelle's, are you? Do you like working there?"

"Yes, ma'am."

"Mr. Sawtelle is rather strict, I've heard."

"I guess so, ma'am. I mean, I've only just started there, so I don't know yet."

"Well, it's a fine thing, building boats," Mrs. Chase said. "Yes, indeed, I'm sure it is. And you're very wise to read some books on the subject." Taking his library card, she stamped it and handed it back to him.

Vinnie thanked her.

"Don't thank me," she said. "Thank whatever you

have in that young head of yours that sent you here."

The funny thing was, he was really eager to read the books. Yes, he was, even though his visit to the library had been a cover-up for calling on Liz Maple. He thought about it as he hurried back to where he'd left the box of groceries.

The box was still in the bull briers. Fishing it out, he hoisted it to his shoulder but decided against trying to go through the woods with it, and headed homeward along the road instead. When he had about a quarter mile left to walk, a pickup truck came up behind him and passed him and stopped.

It was the Camp Wildeway pickup. The man driving it was a handyman at the camp, Ev Hutton. On the seat beside him was the red-headed boy with the freckles, Steve Dennis. Steve stuck his head out and yelled, "Hey, Manuel! You want a ride?"

"Sure!" Vinnie yelled back.

Steve reached down to take the box from his hands and then moved over to make room for it and Vinnie on the seat. "Ev, this is Manuel Correra," he said to Ev Hutton. "He's a friend of mine."

Ev twisted his long, thin face and said, "This is who?"

Vinnie laughed. He had known Ev Hutton since he was old enough to go to the movies. All the kids knew Ev Hutton. He was a loud-talking man with long hair. It was Ev who put up the posters in front of the theater and swept the place out, even selling tickets sometimes. A new man had gotten the movie-house job last year, though, and now Ev worked at the camp.

Vinnie said to Steve, "My name isn't Manuel Correra. It's Vinnie Blake. Ev knows me."

"I knew that wasn't your real name." Steve grinned. "I told you so the day Perkins locked you in the office."

"Hey, now, wait a minute," Ev Hutton said. "Are you sayin' it was Vinnie that Perkins caught in the kitchen that day?"

"It was me," Vinnie admitted.

"That explains it, then."

"Explains what?" Steve said.

"About the stealin'. When I heard that Perkins had caught a kid takin' food, I couldn't figure out why anyone would do such a thing. Now it's easy. When a boy's pa is in jail and his ma has three mouths to feed, I can understand." By now Ev had gotten the pickup moving again. " 'Course, I didn't know Vinnie's pa was in jail at the time. Nobody 'round here did, I guess. I heard about it on the radio sometime after he escaped."

The freckled boy from Camp Wildeway looked with wide eyes at Vinnie. "Is that true? Your father was in jail and escaped?"

Vinnie knew he had to answer somehow. He nodded.

"What was he in for?"

"Well . . ."

"He got into a scrap with somebody, the radio said," Ev Hutton filled in. "He ain't no criminal. It wasn't even a real escape. What I mean, a bunch of others broke out and made him go along so's he couldn't talk. Some of 'em been caught already, and told what happened."

Steve turned himself sideways on the pickup seat and looked at Vinnie hard. "So that's why you needed food," he said quietly. "Are things still bad for you at home? I mean, I have some money at camp. My folks give me spending money."

Vinnie said no, and told about having a job at the boat yard. "But, hey, thanks," he said. "Anyway, I have something of yours I don't think you meant to give me."

"What's that?"

"You wouldn't guess in a million years, I bet. I don't think you even know you gave it to me. A medal."

"A medal?"

"When you gave me the money out of your pocket, it was in with the change. FIRST AWARD, LEADERSHIP, it says."

"Well, I'll be." Steve shook his head. "You know, I did sort of wonder for a while. Not if I gave it to you—I never thought of that. About where I lost it, I mean."

"I wish I had it with me. But I could meet you someplace and give it to you, couldn't I?"

"Sure."

Vinnie thought for a few seconds. "You know that old Injun tree, where the kids on the treasure hunt found my pail of blackberries? Could we meet there?"

"All right. When?"

"How about Sunday?"

"Sunday it is. In the afternoon, when the camp kids are supposed to rest up and write home and stuff. Like about three o'clock?"

"Three o'clock Sunday," Vinnie said, feeling great about it. He really did want to give Steve back the medal, because he was pretty sure you had to work hard to win something like that. And because he would like to have Steve for a friend.

They drove on in silence for half a minute or so and then Vinnie said, "Hey, tell me something. Was Perkins mad when he found me gone?"

Steve laughed. "Was he mad? He almost had a fit!"

"Does he know it was you let me out of there?"

"Uh-uh. He knew somebody must have opened the screen for you, but he never found out who. Funny thing, too—a couple of the kids told me they saw me do it. I mean they saw me open the screen and they even watched you climb out the window. But they wouldn't tell him."

"They must like you," Vinnie said.

"Well . . . but they liked the way you stood up to Perkins, too. They told me so."

"Has he still got it in for me?"

"I wouldn't come too near the camp if I were you. One thing about Perkins—he may be dumb, but he never forgives anyone who makes him look dumb."

Ev Hutton spoke up. "That Mr. Perkins is not the regular camp director, you know. They hired him when Mr. Snow took sick. And if you ask me, they made a big mistake." He turned his head to look at the box Vinnie was holding on his knees. "Where should I drop you off with that, Vinnie? You want me to drive into your yard?"

"Uh-uh," Vinnie said quickly. "I better get off right here."

Ev brought the pickup to a stop. "What's in it, anyway?" he asked as Vinnie jumped down with the two books from the library and Steve handed the box down to him.

"Groceries. Liz Maple had some she didn't want to keep in her store any longer."

"It was real good of her to give 'em to you," Ev said. "But that's just like her."

With a nod to Ev and a "See you Sunday" to Steve, Vinnie stood there with the box in his arms and the books on top of it, watching the truck go on down the road.

Before approaching the house, he hid the groceries at the far edge of the yard, near where he had talked to Pa. Then he crossed over to the house, whistling, so Ma would think he had just come home through the woods as he often did.

The back door opened before he reached it.

"Aren't you pretty late?" Ma said as he went past her into the kitchen.

"I guess I stayed kind of long at the library."

"I guess you did. Did you get any books?"

He handed them to her. "Mrs. Chase found them for me. She said I ought to show them to Mr. Sawtelle before I study them, though, or I might be wasting my time on books that ain't any good."

"Aren't any good."

"Aren't. Can I go over there after supper?"

"Go where?"

"To Sawtelle's. Didn't I just tell you—"

"All right, all right," Ma said. "I was thinking of something else. My goodness. How much walking do you want to do in one day?"

"It isn't far to the boat yard."

"Isn't it?" She made a face at him, but he could tell she was not annoyed. "I'll remind you of that when you complain how tired you are from going over there someday."

"Can I go?"

"We'll see," she said. "Evening's a long way off yet."

He wasn't worried. He had the whole afternoon to soften her up and could do it, he knew, by taking Rosanna outdoors for a while and maybe doing a few extra chores around the house. You could always soften Ma up if she didn't have any real reason to be fretful.

To tell the truth, it was more than he had expected. She could have been real hard to get along with after that visit from the police.

N I N E

When Ma let him out that evening, Vinnie headed for the boat yard with the box of groceries. If he went to see Pa first and talked to Pa as long as he hoped to, it might be too late afterward to call on Clayton Sawtelle.

He couldn't just say he'd been there, either. Ma

was likely to run into the old man somewhere and mention it.

Hiding the box in a patch of grass at the bluff's edge, he went to the back door of the big house and rang the bell. "Are you awful busy, Mr. Sawtelle?" he asked when Clayton opened the door.

"What is it?" Clayton looked surprised.

Vinnie thrust the two books at him. "I got these at the library today, but Ma says before I read them I ought to ask you if they're any good." If he said it was his own idea, Clayton might think he was just trying to act smart.

Taking the books to the kitchen table, Clayton sat and peered at them, pulling at his mouth while he studied some of the diagrams. He took so long over them, Vinnie began to worry about having enough time to go to the cove.

"They're all right," the old man said at last. "How'd you happen to select such good books?"

"Well, it wasn't me, really. Mrs. Chase found them for me."

Clayton nodded. "If you actually study these, I expect you'll learn something."

"That's swell," Vinnie said, more and more worried about the time. "I'll read them. You bet."

"You seem to have an honest interest in boats."

"Yes, sir."

"I'm glad to know it. Is there anything else you want from me?"

"No, sir."

"I'll say good-night, then. I've some accounts to work on."

Vinnie ran past the boat shed to the box of groceries. It was not easy sliding down to the beach with that and the books, but he managed. Fifteen minutes later he was sitting on a bed in the schooner's cabin, watching Pa put the groceries away.

Mostly they were canned goods—corned beef and tuna fish, condensed milk, peas and corn. There were some crackers and a slab of bacon, though, and Pa cut off a sliver of bacon with a knife that was in the box and began chewing on it. He really liked raw bacon, Vinnie remembered. Maybe Liz knew, too.

Along with the food was a bottle that puzzled Vinnie until he caught a whiff of what was in it. Liz had thought of just about everything, it seemed. He hadn't mentioned Pa's lantern, he was sure, but the bottle contained kerosene.

"This must have been pretty heavy for you," Pa said. "I'm proud of you, Vinnie. And I hope you know it was mighty good of Liz to give you all this stuff."

"She didn't give it to me, Pa. She gave it to you."

"Well, all right. She's fond of you, though. She told me so more than once." Pa reached out to lay a hand on Vinnie's arm. Then he said, "What about the police? Have they been around again?"

"No, Pa."

"Your ma say anything about me?"

"Nothing new. Only what she's said before."

Pa cut another slice of bacon. "I guess I can't blame her much for feeling the way she does about me, can I? I mean your ma's a fine woman, son.

Here. You want a piece of this?" He held a piece of bacon out to Vinnie on the knife blade. "You like bacon, don't you?"

Not raw, Vinnie thought, but took it to please him and chewed on it, thinking about Ma. After a while he said, "If Ma's a fine woman, how come she runs you down the way she does sometimes?"

"Well, it's because I don't shape up to her ideas of what a husband and father ought to be like, I guess. I don't fit the mold, so to speak."

"Huh?"

"Look. I'm a carpenter and a pretty good one, okay? So according to your ma's way of thinking, I should work at being a carpenter and forget everything else." Pa breathed out a small sigh and shook his head. "Your ma doesn't seem to understand that a man might need to dream sometimes."

"About going to faraway places, you mean?"

"Well, that could be part of it. But don't let it worry you. Just be glad you've got the two of us in you, if you know what I mean. You and Rosanna both. *Do* you know what I mean?"

Vinnie wasn't sure he did, but said, "I guess so."

"And look," Pa said, "I know things must be pretty tight at home right now, with me not working. But I mean to send your ma money when I'm earning some again. Even if she never wants me back, I'll send money as long as she needs it."

"Sure, Pa."

"Is Rosanna talking now? You didn't say."

"Some. I teach her every chance I get."

"I'm sure you do. I wish I could see her, or even a picture of her. I don't suppose you've acquired a camera in the months I've been away."

Vinnie wagged his head.

"No, I suppose not." Pa rubbed the side of his nose and looked off into space. "You know what you could do, though? You could draw me a picture of her. Now, wait a minute," he went on quickly, holding up a hand before Vinnie could protest. "Don't look as if I asked you to paint a portrait or carve a face out of marble. There's an easy way to do it—a way we used to do pictures of each other in jail, just to pass the time."

Vinnie leaned forward, eagerly listening.

"What you do," Pa said, "is get a sheet of white cloth or paper—paper would be easiest for you, most likely—and fasten it to the wall, then sit the person down in front of it and shine a light on him so his shadow falls on the paper. Then you just trace around the shadow and you have your picture. You have a silhouette, they call it. That'll satisfy me, a silhouette of Rosanna so I can tell what she looks like now. Think you can do it?"

"I guess so. I can try."

"Good. You do that. The big thing is, she has to hold her head still, but I believe you can manage that with a little patience. Now, about the food. When you see Liz again, be sure to thank her for it. I mean, be sure to give her my thanks. You want to go now?"

"Not yet. I don't have to go yet."

"Where are you supposed to be tonight? The Raymonds' again?"

Vinnie told about fooling Ma with the books, and Pa said that was smart of him, though it was a shame he had to do such a thing. Then the whisper of the sea came back, and the creaking of the ship as the waves made her tremble, and Vinnie looked at Pa and was sad.

It wasn't right for Pa to be shut up here, eating raw bacon, when he ought to be home. It wasn't right for him to be sitting here dressed in an old black suit that was too big and made him look foolish. This time of year you didn't usually see Pa in any kind of jacket, and here he was wearing this old black one because the schooner was so cold and damp. It just wasn't right. And it wasn't right for Ma not to be helping him, either. He'd given up Liz Maple to marry Ma, hadn't he? So he loved her, and she knew it.

"Pa?"

"What is it, boy?"

"When you go away, I'm goin' with you!"

"Well, now, I haven't given a whole lot of thought to going away," Pa said. "At least, not yet."

"It don't matter. When you go, you'll need me. You can't handle a boat this big all by yourself."

Pa looked around the cabin, not saying anything.

"We really can fix her up and go away in her, can't we?" Vinnie said, getting scared. "You said we could!"

"Did I say that?"

"You said we could go clear around the world in her!"

"Well, all right, if that's how you remember it."

"She doesn't belong to anyone, does she, Pa?"

"Not now, I guess. She did once, of course."

"Who?"

"Well, when she was abandoned here she belonged to some men in the drug trade. They ran her aground one night trying to give the slip to a government boat that was chasing them. But they got caught and jailed, anyway, and then she just lay here anchored in litigation." Pa reached for the slab of bacon again; he sure liked raw bacon. "Far as I know, they were never able to get all the legalities straightened out, and that's why she's still here. But there's more to her than that."

"More what?" Vinnie said.

Pa had that gone-away look in his dark eyes again that meant he was pondering big things he hoped to do someday. "You know this boat's name, I suppose," he said, folding his arms on his chest.

Vinnie nodded. "It's *Phoenix*." The name was painted in black letters on the stern, and he knew how to pronounce it from hearing the boat talked about. "It's the name of a bird," he added. In school he and some other kids had gotten into an argument about it once, and looked it up in a dictionary.

"That's right." Pa was pleased with him, you could tell. "But not just any bird. The phoenix is a beautiful bird that lives forever."

"A bird can live forever?"

Pa fiddled for a minute with the sleeves of his oversize coat, then took the coat off and tossed it onto the empty bed and sat there in his undershirt. He didn't have on a shirt. "The phoenix can live forever," he said. "Every five or six hundred years he finds a big fire and burns himself up in it, and then he's born again from the ashes. He's immortal. But about this schooner, she may not have been named for that particular phoenix. There's a city of that name in Arizona that I'm pretty sure we don't need to consider, but there's also a cluster of islands called the Phoenix Islands in the Pacific Ocean. Lots of ships are named for islands, I guess you know."

Vinnie nodded.

"Another Phoenix is a star or a cluster of stars in the southern sky. I'm sure if I was naming a boat as fine as this one, I'd give the names of stars a lot of consideration."

Vinnie was disappointed. "So you don't know what the boat was named for?"

"Not if you put it that way, hard as concrete with no bend or give to it, I don't. But if I want to believe she came here from a coral island of that name in the Pacific Ocean, guided by a star of that name in the southern sky, and that she's immortal, I don't know who's to say I can't. Do you?"

Laughing because he felt good now, Vinnie said quickly, "No, sir!" To be truthful, he hadn't given much thought to the name of the boat before, but could see now that *Phoenix* was a much finer name than most boats had. "Pa," he said, "did anybody ever go 'round the world in a boat this small?"

"Lord, yes. There's men been clear around the globe in boats not one fourth as big as this. Alone, too. You ask Nora Chase at the library and she'll show you some of the books they've written about their voyages. A boat this size wouldn't even be risky."

"Do you know anybody who ever went off in a boat like this? Personally, I mean?"

"No, I don't. But I know about them, and I don't see what knowing them in person has to do with it. For instance, there are boats like the *Phoenix* sailing all over the Pacific Ocean, carrying goods and people from island to island. The same in the West Indies. If a man had a boat like this, he could go almost anywhere and make a living—a good living, too—and still be free as a bird."

"Wow!" Vinnie whispered.

Pa didn't look small now with his jacket off. You didn't have to feel sorry for him. With his muscles showing and that far-off look in his eyes, it was easy to picture him standing at the schooner's wheel, taking her wherever he wanted her to go. Looking around, Vinnie could all but see the cabin they were sitting in born again out of dying, like the bird. He could see the walls white and gleaming, the floor scrubbed, shiny new oilcloth on the table, and bright new blankets on the painted bunks. What he saw was so wonderful, he couldn't sit still any longer.

"Pa!" he cried, jumping to his feet. "Can we look around and plan how to fix her up? Can we? Please?"

Pa didn't seem too eager, but hung back for only a few seconds. "Well, I suppose so, within reason. We can't show a light on deck and we don't have much time, but all right." Before getting up, he wrapped the slab of bacon he'd been whittling at. "The truth is, I've looked her over pretty much already. To fix her up in any half-decent kind of way we'd need an awful lot of things that are hard to come by, such as tools and lumber and nails."

"I can get what we need! I mean with Liz helpin' me!"

"Can you? Well, all right, boy. Just so you know it's a big project. It'll keep us seeing a lot of each other, anyway, and talking a lot, and that's what I want."

Vinnie was so excited he could hear his heart thumping. On deck he followed Pa around and it was almost as if they were miles from Cape Cod already, under full sail in the West Indies or the South Seas somewhere. The shore was so dark it wasn't there at all, the waves crashed softly against the ship's side, and the *Phoenix* trembled as if she were really under sail.

"I'll tell you what I'll do," Pa said when they had walked around some. "Between now and the next time you come, I'll write down a list of things we'll need to make her seaworthy. How about that for a starter?"

"Oh, boy! Swell!"

Pa put an arm around his shoulders and drew him close, so close he could feel the cool damp of Pa's undershirt against his face and taste the salt on it. The salt was from being wet with spray while walking around to examine the ship, he guessed.

"Mind you, I don't know where you and Liz will get the things we need," Pa said. "And, Lord knows, I can't go chasing around after them myself. But I'll make up a list."

"We'll get them, Pa!"

"Somehow I believe you will. But you'd better leave now, boy. You've been here long enough."

"It ain't very late, Pa."

"Isn't."

"Well, it isn't."

"Yes, it is. You're only supposed to've gone to Sawtelle's to ask about those books, remember. We can talk another time. You run along now before your ma gets to thinking you're up to something."

Vinnie turned to look toward the dark hole in the schooner's side where his borrowed skiff was tied up. "Can I come tomorrow, Pa?"

Pa thought about it and shook his head. "No, I don't think you'd better. I've enough food to last me awhile, and we don't want people getting suspicious. You wait a day or so."

Vinnie bit back his disappointment. "Well . . . g'night, Pa."

"Good-night, mate," Pa said, holding him gently by the shoulders. "Look after yourself. And don't forget to do that picture of Rosanna for me."

T E N

The skiff for Camp Wildeway had been given a first finish coat of paint and put aside to dry. It stood white and proud in a corner of the boat shed, its place on the sawhorses occupied by another boat that Clayton and Wesley had brought in from the yard. This one was a beat-up old rowboat that belonged to a quahauger. Vinnie's job was to scrape it.

The work was hard. Every so often he had to rest, and when he did, Clayton gave him a suspicious look. The weather had turned bleak and windy during the night, and the old man's disposition matched it. Throughout the morning he prowled about the shed like a caged dog, sniffing and growling. Wesley wasn't taunting him now, just watching him with a wary eye.

About eleven o'clock Clayton suddenly stopped planing a plank, walked over to where Wesley was working at a bench, and said, "I want to have a talk with you!"

Vinnie heard most of what was said, even with the wind gusting over the bluff to rattle the shed windows. The old man was in a temper because Wesley was going off to see some woman instead of doing his share of the work. Or, anyway, because he wasn't doing as much work as Clayton thought he ought to be doing.

"You're a partner in this enterprise, aren't you?" Clayton said loudly. "So why don't you act like one?"

"Is it a sin to want a little recreation now and then?" Wesley retorted in a voice a whole lot less loud.

"Not if you do it on your own time, it isn't. But you—"

"I'm old enough to judge whether or not I'm putting in a day's work, I should think," Wesley said. "In case you haven't noticed, I stopped being a teenager some years back."

"You're old enough to know better, if that's what you mean!"

"I don't want to know better. I don't want you holding my nose to your personal grindstone all the time, either. Has it ever occurred to you that you have a one-track mind?"

"What do you mean, a one-track mind?" the old man shouted.

"You know what I mean. Every blessed thing we do in this shop has to be done your way, even when you know it's holding us back. And that's not all. You expect me to wake up in the morning thinking about boats and go to sleep at night to dream about them, never letting anything else into my life." Wesley's voice, too, was loud now. Really loud. "Well, let me give you something else to think about!" he yelled. "How would you like not to have me here at all? Because that's what's about to happen, right now!"

With that, Wesley walked out of the boat shed as if he meant never to come back, and Clayton, after watching him go across the yard, slumped down on a bench and sat there in silence. Vinnie stole glances at the old man while scraping the boat.

The argument had shaken up Clayton, no doubt of it. He kept wiping his forehead with a handkerchief, though his face was dry, not wet. His skin was the color of putty, and he seemed to have trouble breathing.

Vinnie went on sanding.

Clayton slid backward off the stool and slowly

walked over to him, circling the stern of the rowboat. He watched Vinnie at work. Gruffly he said, "You don't have to rub your hands off. Rest awhile, why don't you?"

Vinnie put down the scraping tool and wiped his hands on his pants, leaving streaks of gray dust. "You're a good worker," Clayton said. "You're not as husky as you might be, but that's not your fault." Vinnie wiped his hands a second time, wondering if he ought to answer.

"I'm going to give you more money and pay you by the week," Clayton said, easing himself down on the end of a sawhorse. "You tell your mother when you go home tonight. She'll be pleased, I expect. She's a real hard worker, kind of like me in a way. I imagine she sets herself a goal in life and won't stand for anyone distracting her from it." He paused, and Vinnie saw that the color was slowly creeping back into his face. "Well, aren't you going to say anything?"

"Yes, sir. I'm glad you're pleased."

"I am pleased. You're a good boy. Funny thing," Clayton went on, "your ma's a farm woman from Canada and your pa's purely a landlubber, far as I know. But there's a feel for the sea in you. How do you account for that?"

"Pa always talked about the sea."

"That's no answer. Your pa talked big about everything, seems to me. No, it's just something you picked up, probably. Anyway, you've got it."

For quite a while Clayton went on like that, between spells of silence. Ma would have said he was wound up. Then, when the day's work was finished, he walked to the house and came back with a cardboard shoe box.

"You'll find a real nice little sailboat in here," he said, thrusting the box at Vinnie. "I made it for my own amusement years ago and you can have it. You'll find a doll, too, for your sister. My wife made that just before she died."

Vinnie opened the box and looked into it. "Thanks, Mr. Sawtelle!"

"Remember," Clayton said. "Tell your ma I'm giving you a raise, and you can work for me as long as you like. You're a good boy. You tell her I said so. And with Wesley out of sorts, you'd better come tomorrow."

Vinnie went home by way of the cove, hoping for a chance to row out to the schooner and talk to Pa, but some of the quahaugers' kids were playing at the far end of the windswept beach. He didn't like the way Clayton had run Pa down. *Talked big about everything.* The old man had no right to say things like that. Yet Clayton had actually done some of the things Pa only dreamed of doing. You had to face up to it.

He'd done them—yes—but that was all. Doing them hadn't made him a better man, had it? Or a happier one.

What was a boy supposed to believe, anyway? If you listened to Ma and Clayton, you'd have to think Pa was a man who would never amount to anything because he did too much dreaming. If you believed Pa, then Ma ought to have a better understanding of things that were truly important. That went for

Clayton, too, Vinnie guessed. People were hard to figure out.

At home, when he told Ma about getting a raise in pay, she surprised him. There was a pan on the stove and she was spooning spaghetti out of it, using a big spoon with holes in it. She swung around to look at him, holding the spoon out in front of her and letting milky water drip onto the floor. "A raise?" she said. "A raise so soon? How much?"

"He didn't say how much."

"But what for?"

"He said I'm a good worker."

Ma laid the spoon on the table and took hold of his arms, squatting down to bring herself to his level. Her black eyes had the bright, polished look that meant she was glad, and the sharp lines had left her face and she was pretty. "I knew you had it in you!" she said. "I just knew it!"

"I didn't do nothin'. Only what he told me."

Ma hugged him before she straightened up again. "I'm proud," she said then. "You tell Mr. Sawtelle I'm proud." Then she took up the shoe box Clayton had given him. "What's this?"

"A doll for Rosanna and a sailboat he gave me, one he made himself."

"Can I look?"

"Sure. Give Rosanna the doll, huh?" His sister was in her high chair.

Ma took the things out of the box and studied them. "Why, they're beautiful," she said. "He must have been in a real good mood today."

"He said I've got a feel for the sea in me."

She looked at him and frowned. "You haven't been talking big, I hope."

"I never said nothin' at all."

"Well, don't. Just do your work and keep your tongue still."

He knew what she meant. Don't be like Pa. He wished she hadn't said it. For a minute he had felt all warm inside, and now the feeling was gone.

During supper, though, it came back. Going into the bedroom, Ma returned with a package done up in fancy red paper and put it beside his plate. "This is for you," she said.

He picked it up and hefted it, puzzled.

"Don't you know what day this is?" Ma said.

He shook his head.

"It's your birthday, Vinnie. You're eleven years old."

It was on the tip of his tongue to ask what difference it made. Pa had always been the one to fuss over birthdays, not her. But the look on her face kept him silent. She was pleased with him and wanted him to feel good, he could tell. She didn't put her arms around him, but she was hugging him with her eyes and voice.

"Go on," Ma said. "Open it!"

He found a green sweater inside the package and Ma told him to try it on. She fussed over him then, making him hold his arms out while she felt his shoulders. After she'd walked around him, nodding, she said, "It fits, thank heaven. You grow so fast I never know what size to buy you anymore."

"It's swell," Vinnie said. "I bet it cost a lot of money."

"Never you mind what it cost."

"But we don't have money for things like this, Ma."

"It's your birthday. I sold something your pa gave me."

"I'll make it up to you, Ma. You'll see."

"You don't have to make it up to me," Ma said. "You're a good boy. You went to work for Mr. Sawtelle when I told you to, and didn't try to wriggle out of it. You're a big help with Rosanna. You're a good boy in lots of ways."

Vinnie was suddenly miserable. There were times when he thought Ma was the most understanding person in the world, and this was one of them. But he was thinking of Pa, too, out there on the schooner.

How could you feel warm and good toward two people who didn't feel that way about each other, even when you knew they ought to?

It was a stormy night. Now and then Vinnie slept, but mostly he lay awake listening to the rain pelting the window over his head. He was afraid for Pa, all alone out there on the boat.

In the morning the air was clear again, but the wind was still strong. Its howling frightened Rosanna and she cried some while Vinnie was gulping down his breakfast. She was crying when he left.

There was no one in the boat shed, so he went across to the house to find out what he was supposed to do. Wesley's car was not in the yard. Clayton came to the back door in flannel pajamas, his face gray and lined, looking as if he hadn't slept much.

"I'll be over later," he said. "You can finish scraping that old boat."

It was near noon when the old man came at last. He didn't say anything, just sat on a stool and looked out a window. Vinnie wondered what had happened. It had something to do with Wesley, he guessed.

At twelve o'clock Clayton stepped over to look at the boat. "You can quit now," he said, then stood with his hands in his pockets, watching Vinnie put the scraping tools and sandpaper away. When Vinnie picked up his lunch, feeling uncomfortable with Clayton watching him, the old man said, "Maybe you'd like to eat with me at the house. It's too windy for you to sit outside today."

"All right." Vinnie didn't want to. He knew he wouldn't feel like eating with Clayton watching every mouthful. But he didn't want to say no, either.

They went to the house together and had lunch at the table in the big kitchen, and Clayton made tea because, he said, they needed something to warm them on such a bleak day. When Vinnie had finished the peanut-butter sandwich and the hard-boiled egg that Ma had fixed for him, Clayton put out bread and sweet butter and strawberry jam and told him to help himself.

"You don't eat enough," Clayton said.

Vinnie hung back.

With a grunt of impatience the old man layered a

slice of bread with butter and jam, and thrust it at him. "Go on, eat! You can't build boats without eating!" Then he lit a pipe and smoked, sitting sideways on his chair and gazing steadily out a window, as if he were listening to the gull-cry of the wind.

Vinnie had finished the bread and jam before the old man spoke again. "Vinnie," Clayton said. "Vinnie Blake."

"What, Mr. Sawtelle?"

"Nothing. Nothing. I was just saying your name to get the feel of it."

Vinnie was puzzled.

"This old house will be lonesome with Wesley gone," Clayton said. "He and I differed on a good many things, but at least he was here to talk to. You suppose your mother would consider keeping house for me?"

Too startled to answer, and then too frightened when he realized the meaning of what Clayton had said, Vinnie could only stare at the man.

"Don't know why she wouldn't," Clayton went on, scowling now. "This is a good house, cool as any on the Cape in summer and a mighty snug harbor in winter. Plenty of room for you and her and the baby. Matter of fact, I've had it in mind for quite a while to hire someone, because even with Wesley here we needed a woman's hand. I believe I'll put it up to her. Now that your father's escaped from jail, he won't dare show his face around here again."

Vinnie didn't want to talk about Pa. He might say something he shouldn't. "Won't Wesley be back?" he said.

"Not if he meant what he said, and I guess he did. You were right there and heard it—how all I think about is work." Clayton screwed his face up, and all but squeezed his eyes shut, but whether he was about to cry or get angry again, Vinnie couldn't tell. "Anyhow, my son no longer lives here," the old man finished. "He's deserted."

"You mean you and Ma would get married?" Vinnie wasn't sure Ma could marry again, having a husband alive, but maybe she could if Pa went away. Still, she wouldn't want to marry a man as old and crabby as Clayton, would she? Even if he did have a big house and probably lots of money.

"Married?" Clayton said in a loud voice. "Married? My Lord, no. I want a housekeeper, that's all. Someone to cook, and keep the place tidy. One wife's enough for any man to have in a lifetime." He began to chuckle, then suddenly tipped his chair back and seemed to be laughing. At least, his body shook and his mouth opened wide, showing a gold cap on one of his front teeth. But no real sound came out.

When he stopped, he let his chair settle back on the floor with a thud and pushed himself up. "All right, let's do our work," he said then. "There'll be time enough later to thrash out our other problem. What I'd better do is drive you home today and have a talk with your mother."

E L E V E N

Vinnie didn't hear all of what was said that evening. He heard the start of it, with Clayton sitting across the kitchen table from Ma and telling her about Wesley's getting mad at him and leaving. But then, when Ma kept glancing at him as if she wished he weren't there, Vinnie knew he could get out.

Squirming a lot and acting fidgety, he waited for her to say something. When she said, "Vinnie, will you please stop that while Mr. Sawtelle is talking to me?" he asked if he could go over to the Raymonds'.

"Yes!" she said. "For heaven's sake, go!"

He couldn't go to the Raymonds', of course; he had to see Pa and tell Pa what was happening. It was kind of too bad in a way, because he'd hardly seen Mary at all since Pa came back, and she must be thinking something was wrong.

All the way to the cove, and while he was rowing out to the schooner, he thought about that and felt bad about it, because he sure didn't want to hurt Mary's feelings. But he just had to tell Pa about Ma and Clayton.

Pa looked sad when he heard, but then shrugged. "Your ma might as well do it," he said. "If things go all right for me, I'll be sending her money from time to time, but unless she wants me back, I can't see myself finishing out that jail sentence. That means I won't be coming back here."

Vinnie felt almost sick all of a sudden. "You mean never, Pa?"

"Well, 'never' is a pretty big word." Pa's face took on a look that made him seem a lot older than he was, maybe because he hadn't shaved in a long time. "Let's just say that I'd go back to jail in a minute if I knew your ma was waiting for me, but I don't feel I could handle it otherwise. How do you feel about living at Sawtelle's?"

"I dunno," Vinnie said, and it was true, he didn't. "It won't matter much, though. You and me'll be going away together when we get through fixing up the boat."

Pa only looked at him.

"If we weren't going away, though, I don't think I'd like it much," Vinnie said. "Sure, it's a big house and we'd have more to eat, most likely, and I wouldn't have to lug water three or four times a day. But there'd be old man Sawtelle as well as Ma telling me what to do all the time. I'd get pretty tired of it, I expect." He shrugged, using his hands as well as his shoulders. "To tell the truth, I don't know as I blame Wesley much for leaving."

"You sound mighty big and independent all of a sudden," Pa said.

"Well, I'm eleven now. Yesterday was my birthday."

Pa rubbed his nose and smiled. "You don't have to tell me. I know. Many happy returns, boy!" Leaning across the table, he put his hand out. "Shake!"

They shook hands.

"I have a present for you," Pa said, "but I have to say it's not finished yet. It took longer than I thought because I've been cooped up here on this boat and—" He slapped a hand over his mouth as if jamming a cork into a bottle. "Now, look at that, will you? I almost went and told you what it is. What kind of a birthday present would it be if I told you about it first?"

"You don't have to give me anything."

"Yes, I do. I have to because I want to."

"Fixing up this boat and going away in her with you will be the best birthday present I ever had. Did you make up a list of the stuff we need?"

"Yes, I did." Pa took a piece of paper from his pocket and laid it on the table. "But I don't believe you ought to carry it on you," he said when Vinnie reached for it. "If you should lose it somewhere or your ma should find it, we'd be in trouble."

Vinnie held the list under the lantern on the bulkhead and studied it. It surprised him at first, it was so short. Then he realized it was short only because Pa had tried to keep it so. "Lumber" could mean all the different kinds of boards Clayton Sawtelle had in his boat shed. There must be a million kinds of nails and screws. And "tools"? Clayton had whole catalogs of nothing but tools.

"Just memorize it to the best of your ability and leave the list here," Pa said. "Actually, we can use almost anything you're able to beg or borrow. But be careful. You don't want anyone to guess what we're up to."

Vinnie read the list over three or four times and put it down. Lumber, nails, screws, paint, tools—he wouldn't have any trouble remembering. "I better go," he said.

He knew his way around the schooner without help now, but Pa went on deck with him, anyway, and for a minute they stood side by side, gazing out to sea. "Did you do that picture of Rosanna for me?" Pa asked then.

"Not yet, Pa. I ought to wait till Ma leaves me alone with her, don't you think? If I try it with her around, she'll ask too many questions."

"Well, yes, I suppose so. Will you be going to the village again soon?"

"I can if you want me to."

"Good. This time you tell Liz Maple I could use some crackers and cheese, and maybe some peanut butter, if she has any to spare. Along with the other things, that is. You tell her I have every intention of paying her back, too, as soon as I get on my feet. Will you remember that?"

"I'll go tomorrow," Vinnie said.

"How do you know your ma will let you?"

"If she's gonna move to Sawtelle's, she'll want me out of the way while she gets things sorted out and packed up."

"I believe you're right. But it may be days before she makes up her mind about moving to Sawtelle's."

"No, it won't," Vinnie said. "Because when old

Clayton wants something, he wants it right away. How do you know Liz will give me more food for you?"

Pa laid a hand on his shoulder. "Don't you worry about that, boy. Liz Maple is a true friend."

"I've decided to do it," Ma said. "Vinnie? You hear? I'm going to keep house for Mr. Sawtelle."

Feeling her gaze on him, Vinnie put down his pencil and turned his head to look at her. It was just after nine in the morning and he was at the kitchen table copying a diagram from one of the books from the library. Copying it would help him understand it better, he had told Ma. That was true, too, but the diagram also contained an idea he and Pa could use in fixing up the cabin of the *Phoenix*. He didn't dare take the book to Pa, though. Aboard the schooner something might happen to it.

"It will be best for all of us," Ma went on when she had his attention. "When Rosanna's a little older, this house will be too small. It's too small now, if we face up to the truth. You like Mr. Sawtelle, don't you?"

"I guess so."

"Well, he's good to you, isn't he?"

Vinnie studied her. She was sitting by the stove with her hands folded in her lap, the way she did when she had important things to think about. He could see she was troubled. Most likely she wasn't sure she wanted to move to Sawtelle's or anyhow didn't want to make up her mind yet, but felt she had to because the old man mightn't ask her again.

"Well," she said, "he *is* good to you, isn't he?"

"He's all right."

Ma was running out of patience. " 'I guess so. He's all right.' Is that all you can think of to say?"

Vinnie shrugged. The truth, as he had pointed out to Pa last night, was that it wouldn't make a whole lot of difference to him whether they moved or not. He wouldn't be around that long.

But would it be all that great, going away with Pa? Never mind what it would do to his insides, having to leave Ma and Rosanna. Would it be all that wonderful living with Pa on the boat, month in and month out? He loved Pa. He was keen about sailing away to far-off places and seeing things a kid on Cape Cod would never get to see. But he loved Ma, too, and Rosanna. What if he never got to see Rosanna again after teaching her to talk and all the rest of it?

"Vinnie," Ma said, "will you please answer me?"

"Huh?"

"Do you want to move to Clayton Sawtelle's house or don't you? Why do I get the feeling you don't want to?"

"I—guess I'm used to being here, that's all, Ma."

"That's no answer. This house is too small and you know it."

Vinnie thought of another thing. If they moved to Sawtelle's it would be like closing the door on Pa, wouldn't it? Pa could never come live with them in Clayton's house. And Mary, they wouldn't be so close to Mary. He could figure out ways to see Mary, though. The real problem was Pa.

He wanted to talk about it but didn't dare. One little slip and Ma would third-degree him, and then it would come out about Pa being on the schooner and all. But he had to say something because Ma was staring at him and waiting. With a shrug, he said, "Well, gee, Ma . . . Pa built this place and I like it."

"You can unlike it, then," Ma said. "If that's the only objection you can come up with, we're going to live with Clayton—at least for a time. We have hardly any money left, and I need what he'll pay me. It isn't every day a woman is offered a job where she can keep her children with her. You stop and think about it."

She was right, Vinnie supposed. He would just have to make the best of it. Anyway, he'd be going away with Pa when they got the boat fixed up. At Clayton's house, Ma wouldn't need him for anything. But Pa would, on the *Phoenix*.

He went to work on his drawing again. Where could he find the lumber he and Pa would need? He was pretty sure Liz would give him the food, but the lumber could be a real problem.

"Vinnie, would it be asking too much for you to pay some attention to me? Just this once?"

"Ma, I heard what you said. We're movin' to Mr. Sawtelle's."

"Tomorrow. Clayton said he'd move us tomorrow if I agreed to come."

Vinnie nodded, gazing into space. Tomorrow was Sunday, so the old man wasn't doing them any special favor. In fact, he probably wouldn't move them any other day. But tomorrow afternoon at three o'clock Vinnie had promised to meet Steve Dennis at the old Indian tree and give back the medal.

Well, he'd get there somehow even if Clayton did move them. About the lumber—Liz Maple bought some of her stuff in wooden boxes, didn't she? Maybe not so much as came in cardboard, but some, anyway. Maybe she'd give him some boxes if he told her what they were for. It wouldn't be as good as real lumber, though.

"Well," Ma said, "what do you think, for heaven's sake?"

"It'll be all right. Ma?" He stood up and looked at her. "You said a while ago I needed a haircut. Can I go to the village? You won't have time to cut it."

"All right," Ma said. "With all I have to do, I'd as soon not have you underfoot. Tell Andy to cut it good and short, so it won't grow back too quick. Here, I'll give you the money." She started for her bedroom.

"I can pay for it, Ma."

Halting, she turned to smile at him. "Well, now, so you can, can't you? You're a wage earner now. Wait, though." Going into the bedroom, after all, she came back with the brown purse she kept her money in. "I'll tell you what. Suppose we each pay half this time, so you won't feel you have to be one hundred percent independent all at once."

Nearing the Raymonds' house on his way to town, Vinnie began to whistle. Then, as he turned toward the gate, the door opened and Mary stepped out.

When she saw who was doing the whistling, she called his name and came running.

She was going somewhere, Vinnie saw. She had on the brown jacket she wore when the weather was poor like this morning. One sneaker wasn't tied yet. "Where you going?" she asked, out of breath. "To the village?"

"Yeah."

"Well, so am I. Wait a sec." She got down on one knee in the road to tie her sneaker. "What are you going for?" she asked, jumping up again like a jack-in-a-box.

"A haircut."

"I have to go to Maple's. We can go together, huh? I haven't seen you in days, Vinnie!"

"We've been kind of busy," Vinnie said.

"I know. I heard my mom and dad talking about it. They said it was in the paper."

"About my pa, you mean?"

"And those others." There was a note of sadness in her voice. "I'm really sorry, Vinnie. We never knew your pa was in trouble. We just thought he went away." She waited for Vinnie to say something, and when he didn't, she reached out and took hold of his hand. "I don't care," she said in the same soft voice. "I really like your pa. No matter what he did, I like him.

"He didn't do anything very bad," Vinnie said.

"I know."

They walked along in silence for a while, because they didn't always have to be talking to feel good with each other. Then Mary told about a crazy thing her new dog had done that morning. While she told him about it he looked at her and thought again how pretty she was, with her hair that looked as if the sun was shining inside it and her eyes like melted chocolate.

Her dog, an English setter, had chased a skunk and gotten sprayed, she told him, and her mother had said, "Tie him up outside, for Lord's sake. We can't have him smelling up the whole house." So Mary did that, and then another skunk came along, she saw it with her own eyes, and this other skunk thought the dog was a fellow skunk or something and tried to make friends with him.

"You never saw anything so crazy in your whole life, the two of them going around in circles and sniffing at each other and then rubbing their noses together," Mary said, laughing. "I'm sure I don't know what would have happened if Ma hadn't looked out the kitchen window and seen it, and then flung the window up and scared the skunk off by yelling at it. My goodness, they might have got together and been lifelong friends!"

"Then people would have come from miles around to see them," Vinnie said, "and you'd have been famous."

Mary laughed, but he had to move out of the road just then, pulling her with him, because a car had come around the bend ahead and was bearing down on them. It looked familiar, even coming on fast that way. When it sped past, he saw it was Clayton Sawtelle's car with the old man himself at the wheel. Vinnie waved, but the car went on past and he guessed Clayton hadn't noticed him. "That was Mr. Sawtelle," he said to Mary. "I work for him."

"You what?"

"I work for him at his boat yard."

"I don't think I'd like that," Mary said.

"Why not?"

"He's kind of weird, Grandpa says."

"Weird? Like how?"

"Well, he's had the most exciting kind of a life, Grandpa says, but all he thinks about is holding his nose to the grindstone and pinching his pennies. You'd never know he's been master of ships that sailed the seven seas, Grandpa says."

"That's what Wesley said, too."

"His son, you mean?"

"Uh-huh. He made it sound pretty bad."

"Well, it is bad, isn't it?" Mary said. "I mean, wouldn't you think doing such wonderful things would have changed him some? Instead of which he's just a grumpy old man who probably doesn't even remember what he did."

Vinnie felt uncomfortable, hearing such things about Clayton and knowing he and Ma and Rosanna would be moving into the old man's house the very next day. He wondered if he ought to tell Mary he was moving, and decided not to. She might just go on and on about Clayton and make him miserable the whole way to the village, when he wanted to talk about other things. Besides, her grandfather couldn't know all that much about the Sawtelles, could he? He sometimes didn't remember even simple things, like what day it was.

They came into the village the back way, through the playground, and walked down past the drugstore and the barber shop. Vinnie should have gone in there but didn't. He liked looking in store windows with Mary. They stopped to talk to Mr. Wendell for a minute in the doorway of his hardware store. Then, in sight of Liz Maple's, Vinnie stopped.

"I better go back for my haircut."

"Shall I come over when I'm done at the store, so we can walk home together?"

"I guess you better not, Mary. I have some things to do."

"I could wait for you."

"I might be a long time."

"Well, all right," she said. "So long."

He watched her go down to Maple's and then went back to the barber shop. She would be on her way home by the time he got his hair cut; he didn't have to worry about that. There was no one ahead of him in the shop, and Andy, the barber, waved him to the chair.

"Ma says to cut it short," Vinnie said.

Andy just nodded. There were times he talked all through a haircut and times he never said a word, and you could tell this was going to be one of the silent times. That was all right with Vinnie. He wanted to do some thinking, anyway, mostly about what it would be like living at Clayton Sawtelle's.

Andy finished tying the apron around him and he

closed his eyes. Then, to the clicking of the scissors and the stroking of the comb, he sort of dozed off and thought about the *Phoenix,* instead.

It was like dreaming, but on purpose.

T W E L V E

*L*iz Maple was in the store this time, waiting on a customer. The customer left and she called Bill Clay from the back room. "Mind the store for a minute, will you?" Liz said. "I want to go upstairs."

Upstairs she sat Vinnie down in his chair and asked him right away how Pa was. "You have to take him some more food," she said. "The other must be finished by now."

"Yes, ma'am. Only he asked if I could get some crackers and cheese, too, and some peanut butter. And he said to tell you he'll pay you back just as soon as he's able to."

"I'm sure he will," Liz said. "Cheese, huh? It's strange, isn't it, the yearnings people get sometimes. Are you fond of cheese, too?"

"Ma doesn't buy it often."

"I don't suppose she does. But you like it, huh?"

"Yes'm. Lots."

"I'll put two slabs of it in the box, then," she said. "One for you and one for him. And some peanut butter. You just wait here a few minutes now, the same as before."

"Liz . . . "

"Yes?"

"Pa says he can fix that old schooner up if I can get him the stuff to do it with."

"What kind of stuff?"

"Well, you know, some boards, maybe. And a hammer and saw and some nails."

Liz sat down again, and the look on her face made Vinnie wonder if Pa had been wrong about her. She sat there gazing at him for the longest time, then said, "What does he want to fix her up for? He can't stay there."

It wouldn't do to tell her Pa meant to sail away in the *Phoenix*, Vinnie decided. "Well, he'll have to live on board her for a while, he says, till the police stop lookin' for him."

"This doesn't make any sense, Vinnie."

Vinnie was really squirming now. "He only wants a few old boards and things. I was thinkin' if you had some old wooden boxes I could knock apart—"

"You can't carry stuff like that through the village, Vinnie. People will be sure you've got your pa hid away somewhere close by and are taking it to him." Liz wagged her head at him. "It's been in the papers about the jail break, Vinnie. Your pa's name and everything. It wasn't when he was put in jail—I guess it wasn't that important—but a breakout, especially with bad criminals, is big news. The whole town is half expecting he'll turn up here."

Not knowing what to say, Vinnie just looked at her.

"Well . . . I'll tell you what I can do," Liz said at

last. "If he really wants this stuff you're talking about, I'll haul it out this evening in my truck. Boards and nails, you say, huh? And some tools." Vinnie nodded.

"All right. Where should I drop it off? A boy your size can't carry that kind of stuff very far, you know." Vinnie did some fast thinking. "You know Dunner Point?"

"Yes, I know Dunner Point. Of course I do."

"So could you leave it up on the bluff above the cove there? Not in the cove itself, Liz. If you leave it anywhere near the quahauger houses, some of those kids might find it. But on the bluff it'll be safe. Starting tomorrow I'll be living right near there, in Clayton Sawtelle's house."

"You what?" Liz stared as if he'd said something like the world would end tomorrow.

"We're movin' over to Clayton's, the three of us. Wesley left, and Ma's gonna keep house there."

"What about your own house?"

"I dunno, Liz." Vinnie had asked himself the same question, and was troubled.

"You can't just walk away from a place," Liz said. "But, of course, this arrangement isn't a permanent thing, is it? It's only for now, while things are so unsettled."

"I sure hope so."

"You say Wesley left? Why?"

"He and the old man had an argument."

"And not the first one, I'm sure," Liz said. "Well, all right. If you're going to be living there, I'll leave the things on the bluff. From now on that's the way we'd better handle this, so the busybodies won't start getting any ideas."

Getting out of her chair, she came over and mussed up Vinnie's hair. Then suddenly she leaned over and kissed him on the cheek. She smelled of lilac blossoms again, and the smell stayed with him most of the way home, reminding him what a swell friend she was.

They moved to Clayton Sawtelle's house the next morning, Sunday, and Vinnie had to admit it was an improvement in some ways, even though he felt as if something was dying inside him. At least he had a real nice room at Clayton's. It was twice the size of his room at home.

"It's not the best in the house, but I guess it's better'n you're used to," the old man said, leading him into it. "I'd give you Wesley's, but if I did that and he came back, you'd only have to move again."

"You mean Wesley might come back?" Vinnie asked. It wouldn't be so bad living here if he had Wesley to talk to sometimes.

"Who knows?" Clayton said. "He walked out once before and came back, so maybe he'll change his mind again." Striding across the pine-board floor, he opened a window. "As I say, this isn't a bad room at all. Come here a minute."

Vinnie went and stood beside him.

"Just look out there, boy."

Vinnie looked down and saw the grass of the yard running green and level to the low stone wall at the edge of the cliff, and beyond that the sea. From this particular window you had a view of almost the whole Atlantic Ocean, it seemed. Of course, it wasn't really the whole Atlantic; he knew that. Nobody could see more than a small part of such a big ocean from any one place. But being able to see so much from your own room was just great.

A window on the other side of the room looked out over the roof of the kitchen and a row of pines between the house and the road.

Clayton seemed glad they had moved in with him, and it was a real nice house, real big. Ma and Rosanna had a room at one end of the upstairs hall, and he had this one next to it, and there were two other bedrooms. One had been Wesley's and the other was Clayton's.

Left alone, Vinnie sat on his bed and looked around. Along with the bed his room contained three chairs and two large bureaus. It had a closet you could walk into, with drawers at one end and a long wooden pole to hang clothes on. All the furniture was maple, the color of honey.

His door was open and he heard Ma coming down the hall. "Well," she said, walking in on him, "how do you feel now about coming here to live? Better, maybe?"

He nodded.

"I should think so," she said. "Don't sit on the bed, young man. It's bad for beds to sit on them. Here you don't have to. We've got chairs enough."

He got off the bed and watched her walk around the room.

"It's nice and clean," she said. "Clayton had our

rooms cleaned for us, he told me. Every stick of furniture was washed with soap and water, then polished. Be sure you keep yours looking like this. You hear?"

"I won't dirty it."

"Of course you won't." She went to the window overlooking the sea, and put her face close to the glass. "My, what a view! It's even better than the one I have. Well, all right." Passing him on her way back to the door, she touched him on the shoulder. "You start putting your things away, and I'll come in later and arrange them the way they ought to be."

Vinnie's clothes were in two cardboard cartons out in the hall, and he had brought a smaller box of really personal things, too—his baseball bat and glove, the harmonica the man at the carnival had given him, and some special things he had saved since he was a kid. He carried the cartons into the room now and began to put things away. In the box of personal stuff was the medal Steve Dennis had given him by mistake.

He looked at it again: the Indian head and the name of the camp on one side, the words FIRST AWARD, LEADERSHIP, STEPHEN DENNIS on the other. For a minute he was back in the camp office, with the freckle-faced boy whispering at him through the window screen. But only for a minute.

With the medal in his pocket he went to stand at a window again, but not to look at the sea this time, just to think how he could get out this afternoon to meet Steve. And how, with Clayton keeping an eye on him, he'd be able to get out again tonight to take the lumber and stuff to Pa after Liz Maple left it on the bluff.

Living at Clayton's was going to make a lot of things harder, he told himself.

T H I R T E E N

When he came in sight of the old Indian tree, Vinnie again recalled how Pa used to talk about it.

"You can learn a thing or two from that tree," Pa said once. "For instance, when the Cape Injuns wanted to mark which way a trail went, they always split and bent a young tree. And you know why they chose a young one? Because they knew it would grow that way and they would always have a trail marker there."

Right now, though, he had something more to think about than Indian lore. He knew he was late and was afraid Steve Dennis might have gotten tired of waiting and gone back to camp.

But that hadn't happened. As he approached the old tree, he saw Steve sitting on the ground at the base of it. Steve saw him at the same time and jumped up.

"Hi!" Steve said, jabbing his hand out. "For a minute there I thought you'd forgot about coming."

"I didn't forget. We moved to a new house this morning and I had a lot to do. Here." Vinnie reached into his pocket. "I brought your medal." Actually, it hadn't been hard to persuade Ma to let him out. He'd only had to suggest it might be a good idea for him to go back to the old house one last time, to make sure everything was locked up.

Steve barely glanced at the medal before putting it into his pocket. "Thanks," he said. "But, listen—I have to warn you about Perkins. Like I told you, he was mad as a hornet when you escaped. He's even madder now because he hasn't been able to find out who opened that screen."

"Okay."

"Be real careful when you come around here. Do you come around much?"

"Well, I used to. I won't now, though."

"I have to watch out, too," Steve said. "I think he suspects I'm the one let you out. In fact, when I left camp a while ago to come here, I looked back and saw him in the office doorway, watching me. So I can't stay and talk to you like I wanted to. I better get back there in a hurry."

"All right."

"So long for now, then. Thanks again for the medal." Steve turned away.

Right then, before Vinnie could even say good-bye, a familiar voice came booming at them like a clap of thunder from a nearby alder thicket. "You, there! Both of you! Stay right where you are!"

Vinnie knew that voice all too well. He'd heard it in the camp kitchen and again in the camp office. Both times it had sent cold shudders through him. Now it almost turned him to ice.

But not for long. Knowing if he got caught it would probably mean the end of his job in the boat yard—and the end of Ma's job, as well—he ducked and ran.

He couldn't look back to see if Perkins was after him. From the road he might have been able to do that without crashing into something, but he didn't stay on the road. He made straight for the blackberry swamp and plunged down into it like a hunted deer.

He knew that swamp. He'd walked about every square inch of it, searching for berries. Maybe it wasn't a real swamp with lots of water, but it had a million holes you could stumble into and more thorns than an army of porcupines had quills. He didn't have to look back. A man like Perkins could never follow him through such a place.

After a few minutes he slowed down, though. If he tore his clothes on the blackberry bushes, Ma would want to know how it happened.

What would they do to Steve? Send him home? But maybe Steve wouldn't mind being sent home. He didn't like the way Perkins was running the camp, anyway.

These thoughts and more buzzed like stirred-up hornets in Vinnie's head as he made his way through the swamp and finally climbed out of it. An open field confronted him then. Crossing it to a dirt road, he trotted down that for half a mile, then cut through some woods and came out in back of his old house, close to where Pa had whistled at him when he went to the well for water.

When he let himself into the house with the key Ma had given him, he found they had left a window unlatched, just as he'd warned Ma they might have. He wasn't surprised, the way Clayton had been stomping around and getting in the way. He latched the window and left, turning for a last look when he reached the road.

He hated to see the house empty. And he was sad at the thought of all the trouble he'd gotten Steve Dennis into.

Going to Pa that night was easy. All Vinnie had to do was wait for Ma and Clayton to go to bed, which they did early because both were tired from the moving. Then he climbed out his window onto the kitchen roof and slid down that to the roof of the woodshed. From there it was an easy drop to the yard. He could get back without trouble.

On the bluff above the cove he found a box of food, some boards, some tools, and even a box with cans of paint in it. Sliding everything down the cliff and lugging it to one of the quahauger boats took quite a while, but he managed.

Pa was pleased.

"As I've said before, Liz Maple is a real friend," Pa said. "Now, this is what we'll do, to be on the safe side and not run any risk of trouble. You row ashore and go down the beach toward the quahauger houses, and when you've had time enough to get there, I'll do some sawing and hammering. You listen hard with both ears. We have to be sure the sound won't carry that far and give us away."

"It won't, Pa."

"No, I don't think it will. But the wind is blowing that way, and we ought to make certain."

Vinnie went ashore and walked down the beach. It was a dark night, so dark he couldn't even see the fiddler crabs he disturbed, though he could hear them scuttling through patches of dry seaweed. He listened hard for sounds of hammering and sawing but couldn't hear a thing through the whistle of the wind and the noise of the sea among the rocks. There were quite a few big rocks at that end of the cove and the sea made a lot of noise, he was glad to find out. "You could fire a gun off and nobody'd hear it," he reported to Pa.

"Then we'll go to work," Pa said. "We'll start right now to raise this *Phoenix* of ours from the ashes."

The next couple of hours were special. They worked on the boat, but it didn't seem like work to Vinnie—not with Pa singing songs, reciting poems, and talking his head off. Vinnie sang along when he happened to know the song or could catch onto it quickly enough, and he listened in wonder to the poems. There was a scary one about a schooner named *Hesperus*, which got wrecked on a reef called Norman's Woe. And one about Paul Revere that Pa didn't know all of, but what he knew was exciting. And there was a really funny one about two fellows named Abdul A-bul-bul Ameer and Ivan Skavinsky Skavaar who had a big fight. Pa even knew some music to that one and after reciting it, he sang it.

"You know," Vinnie said, "when we had to memorize a couple of poems in school, most of us kids thought it was a waste of time. Now I can see why it wouldn't be."

They worked on the cabin, painting. "There's a hole in her up forward that I thought we might start to patch," Pa said, "but while you were ashore I looked at this paint Liz left and had a change of mind. She doesn't sell paint in her store, so this must be some she had around the house, and I swear there aren't this many colors in a rainbow. It's beautiful, that's what it is. So what we ought to do when you're here, it seems to me, is paint. There's a whole lot of inside painting to do. I can manage the carpenter work myself."

Vinnie started on the bed Pa said was to be his. He wanted the wooden part of it white and the wall behind it blue, but first he had to borrow Pa's knife and scrape off some old gray paint that was on both. Pa started putting some white paint on the opposite wall.

"You remember the time we built the crib for your sister?" Pa said while they worked.

"You bet. And you painted her name on it."

"That was the first time we really worked on anything together, if my memory serves me right. I thought about it a lot afterward. In fact, I always thought of the two events together—Rosanna being born and us working together on that crib for her."

"And going to Sagamore," Vinnie said. "That was part of it, too. The man giving us the harmonica."

"Yes, and that, too. There's a lesson to be learned in that, boy. I bet you can tell me what it is if you think about it."

Vinnie thought hard but had to admit he couldn't see what Pa was driving at.

"Would you say that was a big thing we did, making a crib for Rosanna?" Pa asked.

"You bet!"

"No, it wasn't. The baby had to have something to sleep in, sure, but what made the crib special was the love we put into it, wanting it to be the most beautiful crib in the world because it was for her. The same goes for the harmonica, in a manner of speaking. It wasn't any extra-fancy harmonica, but the man gave it from the goodness of his heart. That's why you remember it."

Vinnie thought again and nodded.

"I'm real pleased you remember that harmonica," Pa said. "It's a good sign."

"I still have it."

"I'm sure you do. Can you play it?"

"Some."

"Why don't you bring it here next time you come, then? We can have us some music between spells of painting."

"What if somebody heard us?" Vinnie said.

"We don't have to make a whole lot of noise to feel good about it," Pa said. "Besides, you couldn't hear me hammering."

They worked for about two hours altogether, and then Pa said they ought to quit. "You run along now or you'll be so bleary-eyed in the morning, they'll suspect something. It's good you can get out at night and come here, but we have to be careful. Clayton Sawtelle is nobody's fool."

Even so, Vinnie didn't hurry to get home after putting the borrowed skiff back with the others. Not even a little bit tired, he walked slowly along the deserted beach in the dark, telling himself he was exploring some far-off island that he and Pa had discovered in the *Phoenix*.

F O U R T E E N

*H*e saw Pa almost every night after that, but it was going to take a long time, Vinnie realized, to put the *Phoenix* in shape for going away. And of course he wasn't always sure he wanted to go away, even with Pa. He wasn't sure, either, that Pa himself wanted to go away.

They both had a whole heap of thinking to do yet. But until the thinking was done, it was just great to be working and talking with Pa. And they weren't hurting Ma or Rosanna by doing that, were they?

In the meantime, he had problems at home.

Things fooled you. The one thing he'd been sure he would like better at Sawtelle's—not having to walk so far to work in the morning—didn't really amount to much, after all. There were worse things than walking, he discovered. There was the feeling of being cooped up in one place all the time with Clayton watching him.

He missed the old house, too.

"You're late," Ma said when he got home from one

of his trips to town. "What happened? Did you forget your way here?"

"I came around by our old house."

"You what?"

"I came back the old way."

Ma was peeling potatoes at the kitchen sink. Turning to face him, she stood there with her wet hands backward on her hips and looked at him as if he'd said something that scared her. "Now, why in the world would you do a thing like that?"

"I dunno. I just felt like it."

"You just felt like walking all that way when you didn't have to? Did you go into the old house?"

"No. I gave you back the key, remember?"

"Well, did you feel homesick? Is that why you came that way?"

"I told you, I dunno why I did it."

"Did you visit anyone?"

"I stopped at the Raymonds' awhile."

The scared look went off Ma's face and she began to smile, not at him but to herself. She smiled and nodded and then said, "I see. What you're trying to tell me, or trying not to tell me maybe, is that you visited Mary Raymond. Is that it?"

Behind Vinnie, in the kitchen doorway, Clayton Sawtelle's voice said "Mary Raymond?" and Vinnie turned, startled. He hadn't known Clayton was standing there. The old man wore a carpenter's apron with some wood shavings clinging to it like leaves to a window screen, and had a plane in one hand. He must have just come across from the boat shed.

"The Raymonds were neighbors of ours," Ma said, answering him. "Mary's their daughter."

"I know who she is," Clayton grunted. "She's Obadiah Raymond's granddaughter. I've seen Vinnie with her, too."

Vinnie nodded, remembering the time he'd been walking to town with Mary, and Clayton had passed them in his car. He didn't like the way Clayton was looking at him, though.

"She's a lovely girl," Ma said.

The old man's skimpy eyebrows arched up the way they did sometimes when he chose to let them talk for him instead of saying "Well!" or "Is that so?" Then he scowled and said, "I know that. It's her grandfather I'm not too fond of."

"Why? What's he done to you?" Ma said.

"Hasn't done anything. But he makes remarks about me, I'm told."

There was a twinkle in Ma's eyes. "Remarks you don't deserve, you mean? Or is it because you deserve them and know it that you're so touchy about him?"

Clayton grunted again and muttered something under his breath that Vinnie couldn't hear. The look on his face was one Vinnie had learned to be wary of—a tightened-up look that meant he was displeased and was deciding what to do about it.

Still, you couldn't be sure, could you? The old man might be just kind of scared. He'd been acting as if he wasn't certain it had been wise of him to bring strangers into his house. There'd been a holding back about him, a look on his face almost of panic at times.

That could have been it, because a change took place in Clayton the very next day. Vinnie was in the kitchen with Ma and Rosanna, eating his breakfast. Clayton had finished already and gone to the boat shed. The baby was in her high chair. Ma was warming milk for her at the stove. Vinnie was watching her and wondering how he was going to make the shadow picture Pa kept asking for.

Nobody was talking, not even Rosanna. She was just making noises by banging her feet against her chair.

Clayton came in then, wriggling his arms out of an old slicker he'd put on because it was wet out, and Ma turned her head to look at him. "You're damp," Ma said. "Why don't you take that shirt off and let me dry it, Clayton?"

That was all. That was all Ma said. And Rosanna stopped banging her feet and looked at the old man and said, "Clay-ton!" She said it again—"Clayton!"—then clapped her hands at the sound of it coming out of her mouth.

All the starch went out of Clayton. He turned and looked at her as if he'd just been handed a million dollars. "Well, listen to that!" he said, then walked over to the high chair and stood there pulling at his ear and blinking at her. "Did I hear you speaking to me, young lady?" he said.

Rosanna reached out with one hand and grabbed his shirt. "Clay-ton," she said again, not so clearly this time. It was as if she was talking to herself the way she mostly did, but it was plain enough to please him.

"Well, I never," he said, and held a finger up in front of her to see if she would grab it.

She did, of course. She would grab anything she could reach, even if it burned or stung her.

Clayton was already calling Ma by her name, instead of "Mrs. Blake," and Ma seemed to like it. She seemed to like it so much that Vinnie wondered if she was forgetting Pa. He didn't think she could be, though—not when she had Rosanna and himself right under her nose to keep reminding her about him.

Sure, she didn't talk about Pa anymore. When she'd first heard he was out of jail, she had talked some about what she would do if he showed up, but that was over with now. For all she or the police knew, he could be a million miles away.

Her being so friendly with Clayton troubled Vinnie. He stopped sitting with them in the front room evenings and went up to his own room instead. Up there he could be by himself, thinking about Pa while Ma and Clayton talked to each other. Ma didn't need him anymore; he could see that. Not in this house, at least.

But he liked being alone in his room. He always knew he would be climbing out the window later, when Ma and Clayton were asleep, and going down to the cove to work with Pa on the schooner.

Toward the end of that first week at Clayton's, he was lying on his bed one evening with a book from the bookcase downstairs, waiting for Ma and the old man to come up to bed so he could sneak out, when his door opened without any warning and Ma walked in. She shut the door and sat on the bed and looked at him. It was all right for her to sit on the bed, it seemed, even if he wasn't supposed to.

"Vinnie?"

Something was wrong, he guessed. She hadn't come into his room after supper before. "What, Ma?"

"Is something troubling you? If there is, I want to know about it."

"Nothin's troublin' me, Ma."

"You spend an awful lot of time up here by yourself. Every evening now you come up here and shut your door like you don't want to sit in the same room with us."

"I got things to do, that's all."

Ma frowned at him. "Are you lonely, like the day you stopped at our old house?"

He shook his head. "I don't miss the old house, Ma." That was a lie, but not a big one. What hurt was knowing that Pa would never be coming home to them in that house. And maybe he missed the feeling he'd had there that he was important. In that house if something needed fixing after Pa left, like the time Rosanna threw a dish through a window, he was the one supposed to fix it. Clayton did all those things here.

"What is it, then?" Ma said. "Aren't you happy living here with Clayton?"

"It's all right."

"Then will you please tell me what's going on? You used to talk to me about all sorts of things. Sometimes back home you talked so much I was tempted to take you out and drop you down the well."

Vinnie had to laugh.

"That's better," Ma said. "Now tell me."

"Honest, Ma, there's nothin' the matter. You don't need me around the way you used to, that's all. Can't you see?"

"Is it because you miss your pa? Is that why you're—why you want to be by yourself so much?"

"I dunno. I miss him, sure. But if you don't want him back—"

"Vinnie, did I ever say that? In so many words did I ever say I don't want him to come back?"

"That's what you told the police," Vinnie said. "I was right there when you said it."

She got off the bed and stood there looking at him. She looked at him so long he began to be scared. At last she reached down and touched him on the hand. "You make it sound as if everything's been decided till the end of time," she said then. "Like it was something in a book, all written down and finished. It isn't like that, Vinnie. Not many things in real life are forever."

"I don't know what you mean, Ma."

"Things change. Maybe I did say that to the police. Maybe I even meant it at the time. Now I don't know. But we're doing all right here, aren't we? I mean, I have a job, and I have you and Rosanna here with me, and for once in my life I don't have to be worrying all the time. Let's leave it like that for now, huh?"

Vinnie didn't answer.

"So . . . good-night, Vinnie," Ma said.

"Good-night, Ma."

When the door closed behind her, he reopened his book and tried to read some more of it, to kill time until he could sneak out to Pa. But the words kept blurring on the page and finally he just lay there with his eyes closed, thinking about what Ma had said.

You never could tell about people, he thought. Not really. Just when you were sure you had everything sorted out, it turned out you still had lots more to learn.

The next day was one of the hottest of the summer. The cool spell with its showers had passed. The sea was dead flat with a greasy look, and there wasn't a whisper of breeze to stir the grass at the bluff's edge.

Clayton was sanding a second skiff for Camp Wildeway. The camp people hadn't come for the first one yet—it was over against the wall on a pair of sawhorses—but it seemed they had ordered two, not one. The stencil Vinnie had put together that first day was hanging on a nail over the workbench where Wesley had shown him how to clean it. Clayton had decided to wait until they could use it on both boats at the same time.

The old man stopped work and turned to look

out the open door, fishing a red handkerchief from his hip pocket and mopping his face with it. "I need a breath of air," he said. "Come along if you want to."

He walked out of the shed and across the yard to the edge of the bluff, with Vinnie after him. It sure was hot. Ever since lunchtime Clayton had been sanding, and the wood dust was down inside Vinnie's shirt, making him itch. He stood alongside Clayton at the top of the bluff, looking down at the oily-smooth water and scratching himself. Just then Ma came out of the house and let the screen door slam, and it was like a rifle shot, the air was so still.

"Come on," Clayton said. "We'll go along the cliff a ways."

He started off toward Dunner Point, and Vinnie worried about Pa on the schooner. Every night Pa talked about the work he did during the day. Vinnie had seen only what was done in the cabin, because it wasn't safe to go prowling with a light at night, but Pa must be moving around a lot and taking plenty of chances. It would be awful if Clayton saw him.

The old man trudged along the cliff through the heat, wiping his face now and then with the red handkerchief but not saying anything. Down below, the shore changed from beach to black rocks and then back to beach again. It was the cove beach now, with a long line of seaweed baking in the sun and the schooner out there looking, Vinnie had to admit, as if nobody had done a lick of work on her.

"I see the old *Phoenix* is still here," Clayton said. "I haven't been down this way in ages."

"I guess nobody comes here much except the quahaugers."

"That's true." With a hand over his eyes to block out the glare, Clayton peered down at the boat. "*Phoenix.* Now that's a likely name for a fisherman, isn't it?" There was a sneer in his voice.

"Was she a fisherman?" Vinnie said. "I heard she came from the Phoenix Islands in the South Seas."

Clayton made a snorting sound. "Who on earth told you that?"

"I dunno. I heard it somewheres. A long time ago, I guess."

"Well, there may be some islands of that name in the South Seas, but this *Phoenix* we're looking at came from Plymouth, Mass. She was just a fishing boat until some not very smart dope runners took her over."

Vinnie couldn't let it end like that. "Well, anyhow, she looks as if she could have come from the South Seas," he said. "She's real pretty."

"You've been reading too many of those books of mine."

"You've read 'em, too."

"Yes, I have. But I'm old enough to know most of them are pure romantic nonsense, which I guess you're too young to realize yet. If you've got to be romantic, for heaven's sake pick on a proper subject, not a broken-down old fishing boat. *Phoenix,* indeed!"

It was a letdown after all the wonderful things Pa had said, but Vinnie shook it off. The truth probably lay somewhere in between Pa and Clayton, he guessed.

There was no sign of Pa, thank the Lord. He was probably sleeping, figuring on making up for lost time tonight when it wouldn't be so hot.

"By the way," Clayton said, "it's a good thing I didn't give you Wesley's room. He'll be coming home in a few weeks."

Vinnie stopped walking and just stared at him.

"Uh-huh," the old man said. "I phoned him and asked him to come home. Seeing you and your ma and Rosanna together made me feel—well, long as my son's willing, I'd like to have him with me, maybe even on his own terms. What are you staring at?"

"Nothin'," Vinnie said quickly. "Will we still be livin' with you, Mr. Sawtelle? Ma and Rosanna and me, I mean."

"Of course. With Wesley back, I'll need a house-keeper even more. Don't know how I ever managed without one." The old man laid a hand on Vinnie's shoulder. "And you know something, boy? I don't know how I managed in the boat shed without you, either."

FIFTEEN

*T*here was a kind of magic about the cove at night, Vinnie had discovered. It never looked the same twice in a row. It never even smelled or sounded the same.

Some nights there would be almost a gale blowing, and the air would be full of spray and sand. He would have a terrible time launching a boat in such a wind. The surf would slam it into him or tear it out of his hands, half drowning him.

Other nights the cove was a gentle place, no wind to speak of, and the sea so calm you'd swear you could walk on top of the water clear out to the schooner.

The beach was alive on nights like that. A million crabs scurried around on it. Clams spat up through the sand when you walked where they were. You heard the water whispering, the crabs clicking their claws, even seaweed bladders popping and hissing when you stepped on them.

Tonight the sea was quiet, with hardly any swell and only a thin line of froth shining white on the dark sand. The schooner lay out there as if nobody had set foot on her in a thousand years. But when he launched a boat and rowed out to her, Pa was right there as usual, waiting to give him a hand aboard.

"I've got something for you," Pa said when they were inside the cabin. "Here." And he reached under a bunk and brought out a board.

It was no ordinary board, though. It was a piece of thick pine about two feet long with the name VINCENT carved on it in beautiful letters. Vinnie was so surprised he could only hold it and look at it, unable to say a word.

"You didn't forget the way we painted your sister's name on her crib that night," Pa said, "so I decided to do something of the same sort for your birthday.

You can put it up over your bed here."

Vinnie leaned over what would be his bed and propped the board against the wall to admire it. "Thanks, Pa! Thanks! It's great!"

"Speaking of your sister," Pa said, "did you do that shadow picture for me yet?"

Vinnie had to shake his head. "I'm scared. If Ma or Clayton was to start askin' me questions, I might say somethin' dumb."

"Tell them you read about it in a book and just wanted to try it."

"Well, all right."

"I'm hoping for a real fine picture that we can put up in the cabin here."

Vinnie looked around. Pa hadn't done anything yet to the outside of the *Phoenix*, of course. It wouldn't be safe to do that until they were away from here. But every time he came, the cabin was a little different, a little more wonderful than the time before. The two of them worked on it together almost every night, but Pa wasn't satisfied with that; he worked on it by himself in the daytime, too. He wanted it to be beautiful, the way Rosanna's crib had been beautiful.

That's what the cabin was like, when you thought about it. It was like Rosanna's crib, only a lot bigger and fancier because Pa had gotten all those different colors of paint from Liz Maple and had so much more space to decorate. There were waves and circles and lines of color all over the walls, running every which way, so that if you looked long enough you could find almost anything you were able to think of.

Over Pa's bed, for instance, was a mountain with a sun rising behind it, only if you didn't want to think it was that, you could say it was a space ship coming from another world. Each cupboard door was a different color and had different designs on it. The ceiling was the kind of thing you saw when sunlight came pouring in through a church window.

One thing worried Vinnie, though, and he put it into words. "Pa, with you doing all this painting, what about the other work that needs to be done? I mean, shouldn't we be getting the boat fixed up to sail away in?"

"Don't you worry about that," Pa said. "Everything's coming along fine."

"But—"

"Look at this." Pa opened a cupboard door that was a beautiful bright blue with yellow stars all over it. "You know what this is?"

Vinnie saw some folds of old, stained canvas with metal rings in them and felt his heart beat faster. "Sails, Pa? Honest?"

"One, anyway."

"Hey, wow!"

He had been wondering what they would do about sails. You couldn't make them out of just any old thing, and he'd found out from talking to Clayton Sawtelle that they had to have a lot of special fittings. Pa and he could have used an engine on a boat like the *Phoenix*, he guessed, but where would they find one? Besides, it wouldn't be so much fun using an engine. The *Phoenix* ought to have sails. Pa's getting this one was a real big thing, even if what he'd found wasn't new.

"Will one be enough, Pa?"

"No, it won't. But it will get us out of here when the time comes, and that's the important thing. We can't fix her up the way we ought to until we get to someplace where I'll be safe from the police."

"Where'd you get the sail, Pa?" Vinnie knew it couldn't have come from Liz Maple. Liz brought only the things he asked her to.

Pa leaned back and looked like a wise old owl. "Oh, I know where to find a few of the things we need. I even know where I can get us a pump, I think."

"A pump?"

"Certainly, a pump. When I get through patching the holes in this ship, she's got to have the water pumped out of her. She's stuck in the sand and won't come off the bottom until it is. We're not ready for that yet, though."

"Are we gonna work tonight, Pa?"

Pa thought about it and shook his head. "To tell the truth, I'm a little tired tonight. I worked pretty hard all day. Suppose you sit there on your bed and tell me what you've been up to."

Vinnie told about Wesley's coming home, and about giving the medal back to Steve Dennis.

"Steve sounds like an all-right kind of boy," Pa said.

"Yeah."

Pa started talking then about where they might go when the *Phoenix* was ready. "What we could do," he said, "is head for Jamaica first. From there we can run over to Haiti and drop anchor at Cap-Haïtien and climb up to the Citadelle. That's a fantastic fortress on a mountaintop, built years ago by King Christophe, and it's said to be one of the wonders of the world. And we ought to visit that island off the north coast of Haiti where the buccaneers used to hang out in the days of the Spanish Main—Tortuga it was called then. Offhand I'd say it will take us a month or more to do Haiti right, before we can move on to other islands in the Caribbean."

Vinnie felt a touch of awe. "Pa, do you know lots of far-off places that good?"

"Well, I know *about* quite a few places, from books."

"We never had any books around the house, Pa."

"No, because your ma kind of felt it was a waste of time. What I mean, if I brought home a book on carpentry or something of that sort, fine, provided I got it from the library and didn't spend our good money on it. But other kinds of books—well, the truth is, they scared her a little, I think."

"You read them in the library, you mean?"

"Sort of. Not in the library, actually, but I got them from there, most of them."

"I want to go to Africa," Vinnie said. "I read a book about Africa once called *The River of Darkness* by a man named William Murray Graydon. Some fellers went down an underground river on a raft, and never knew where the river would take them or even if they'd get out alive. It was a wonderful story."

Pa studied him and nodded. "Uh-huh. I haven't read that one, but I can see what you mean. About the river, and not knowing where it would take them, I mean."

"Aren't we going to do any work at all tonight, Pa?"

"I think not," Pa said. "I've already done a lot today, as I told you. I carved most of your name on that board, too. More than that, though, I think we ought to just sit here and get to know each other. I'm enjoying this."

Vinnie was enjoying it, too. He lay back on his bed with his hands clasped behind his head and studied the board Pa had carved for him. It sure was beautiful against the painted wall. They talked, and he looked around the cabin again, admiring all the colors. There probably wasn't another ship's cabin in the whole world that was painted like this one, he thought.

For the best part of an hour they talked about places they would go when the *Phoenix* was ready, and what they would do there, and how they would earn money.

They wouldn't need a whole lot of money, Pa said. Only enough to keep the boat in condition and buy a few things for themselves. "Food won't be much of a problem. We'll be catching fish all the time we're at sea, and crabs and lobsters and things like that when we're at anchor. In the tropics we can pick oysters right off rocks and mangrove roots. Then, if we decide to stay on some of those uninhabited islands for a time, like Robinson Crusoe, we'll be able to hunt wild pigs and goats."

It was like a dream.

"How about a tune or two on your harmonica?" Pa said.

Vinnie took the harmonica from the cupboard where he kept it and played awhile. Pa sat there with his eyes half closed, tapping a foot in time to the music.

"Like I said before, you're all right with that thing," Pa said. "Yes, sir, you play it real well."

"I'll get better when we're at sea. I'll have lots of time to practice then."

"So you will."

Vinnie played a little longer and then Pa said, "You hungry? How about an apple?" Opening the cupboard where he kept his food, he pulled out a paper bag and tossed Vinnie a big red Baldwin.

Vinnie almost missed it—not because he couldn't catch an apple tossed at him from only a few feet away, but because of what he saw in the cupboard. It was a lady's handbag and it belonged to Liz Maple. He'd seen it in her apartment lots of times.

It took him a few seconds to get over being startled. Then he bit into the apple and chewed a mouthful while thinking. That handbag could mean only one thing: Liz Maple had been here on board the *Phoenix*. She must have left it by mistake. So why hadn't Pa said she was here?

He didn't stay long after that. It wasn't so much fun anymore, sitting there in the painted cabin and listening to Pa talk about the things they would do together. He wasn't so certain he wanted to go with Pa now. Maybe he hadn't ever been really sure. How could he leave Ma and Rosanna, knowing he might never see them again?

On the way home he though about it, and back in his room at Clayton's he lay awake for hours trying to figure it all out. Pa should have told him about Liz being on the schooner. It wasn't right for partners to keep secrets from each other.

But maybe it was his own fault, for not asking. Most likely Pa would have explained Liz's visit in a minute if he'd asked about it instead of sitting there tongue-tied.

S I X T E E N

A fter breakfast the next day, Clayton went off in his car to a place near Harwich to look at a yawl that had been damaged in a storm. The yawl's owner wanted him to repair it. "I probably won't be back till late afternoon," Clayton said, and told Vinnie to put a coat of paint on a rebuilt sailing pram.

It was a long morning and Vinnie's thoughts kept pulling at him, keeping him off balance and edgy. He wanted to think about the *Phoenix* and what Pa had said about sailing her to the West Indies. The feeling you got from such thinking was the kind you got from reading books, only even better. But every time he began to get into it, he would remember Liz Maple's handbag.

He could imagine what had happened. Liz and Pa had been talking on board the boat, and she'd forgotten the bag when she left. By the time she remembered, she was either ashore or on the way to shore in the boat she'd borrowed, and didn't feel like going back for it. If she'd been aboard the *Phoenix* once, she was probably planning on more visits, anyway.

In the afternoon he finished the pram, and Ma asked him what else he was supposed to do. When he told her Clayton hadn't left any orders, she said he could go to the village for her. "I need some black yarn to mend some of Clayton's socks with," she said, "and I'm sure he won't mind if you take time off for such an errand. Especially if you don't have any work to do."

In the village he went and bought the yarn first, then hurried down to Maple's. Liz wasn't in the store, so he climbed the stairs. He had to knock more than once because a radio was turned up loud inside. He heard it being turned off, and Liz came to the door in her old blue robe.

"Well, hello there," she said.

Now that he was actually here, Vinnie was a little scared. "Can I come in, Liz?"

"Can you come in? Of course you can! You don't expect me to entertain my favorite company out here on the landing, do you?"

He walked in and sat down, and Liz went and got him some milk and cookies from the kitchen. "Now," she said, "suppose you tell me what's troubling you. Something is. I can tell."

"Nothing's troubling me, Liz."

She sat down and leaned forward to peer at him. "Don't you try to fool Liz now."

"Well, nothing much. Ma sent me to town for some yarn, so I thought I'd come and see you."

"And I'm glad you did. But there's something on your mind all the same."

Vinnie chewed on an oatmeal cookie and looked around the room, trying to think how to say it. He wasn't still scared, exactly. He had been at the start, but even a short time in this room, with Liz sitting here facing him in her old blue robe, was enough to put him at ease. He didn't want to say it wrong, though, and give her the notion he disapproved.

"Liz . . ."

She waited for him to go on, but he couldn't. Then she said gently, "Now, what is it? What's happened that you can't even talk to Liz about it?"

"It's you and Pa."

She frowned, but not in annoyance, more as if she wondered what he was getting at. "What about your pa and me?"

"You went to see him on the boat."

Reaching for a cookie from the plate beside him, Liz put it in her mouth. He remembered she had told him once she always ate when she had problems; that was why she'd gotten bigger than she wanted to be. Chewing, she looked at him in silence

138

awhile and then nodded. "Yes, I went to see him. Is there something wrong with that?"

"He didn't tell me."

"Oh? And you feel he should have. Is that it?"

"Well, he and I are supposed to be partners—"

"Vinnie," Liz interrupted, "come here. It's time we had a little talk, and I can't talk the way I want to with you over there."

He slid from his chair and went to stand in front of her.

"Your pa loves you, Vinnie," she said. "He always has. You must know that."

"He likes me all right, I guess."

"Uh-uh." Liz shook her head hard. "Your pa *loves* you, and always has. He was bound to come here to see you when he escaped from jail. I'm only a little surprised he didn't walk right into the house to see your ma and Rosanna, as well, to tell you the truth. He loves them, too."

"Ma?"

"Most of all your ma. I suppose you think because she changed toward him he stopped loving her. But he didn't and he won't."

"You and Pa must be real good friends for you to know so much about him," Vinnie said.

"That's right, we are. I'm probably the best friend your father ever had—or did I tell you that before? But there's only one woman he ever truly loved, and that's your ma."

Vinnie thought of how Pa used to come up behind Ma and put his arms around her, pressing his face against hers and telling her she was the most beautiful woman God ever created, and meaning it, too, you could tell. Then he remembered what Ma had told the police.

And then—it was like grabbing at a board or something when you thought you were drowning—he remembered what Ma had said in his room at Clayton's: *Maybe I did say that. Maybe I even meant it at the time. But now I don't know.*

"Right now, if you were to ask me," Liz said, "I'd guess they're both having problems with how they feel about each other. But underneath those mixed-up feelings they love each other, and don't you forget it for a minute."

Vinnie couldn't think of anything to say to that. Instead, he said, "Did you like the way we fixed up the *Phoenix?*"

"Very much," Liz said. "And it's good for your pa to be working like that, I think. While he's making up his mind what he ought to do, I mean."

"You're the one got the sail for him, aren't you?"

Liz nodded.

"And the pump we need—will you be getting that, too?"

"If I can."

"I don't know why he didn't tell me you went to see him."

"Don't you?" Liz smiled. "It was because I asked him not to."

"But—"

"You might have thought he was cheating on your ma, Vinnie. I couldn't have that."

Vinnie suddenly felt good again. "When the boat is all fixed up, we're going away in her together," he said. "I mean, he is for sure, and I'll go with him now I know Ma and Rosanna don't need me. We'll be going to the West Indies first and then all over. Did Pa tell you?"

It seemed a long while before Liz was ready to answer that. Then she said, "Vinnie, let me say one thing. If you find you can't go—if anything should come up to prevent it—will you promise me something? Will you promise me it won't be the end of the world for you?"

"Well, like I said, since Ma and Rosanna don't need me, I don't know what can stop us," Vinnie said. "Especially with you helping us."

"Oh, my Lord," Liz whispered.

"Huh?"

"Nothing. Never mind."

It was late when Clayton got back that evening. Ma had put his supper in the oven to keep it warm, and she sat with him while he ate. Then she stayed in the dining room, talking with him about Wesley, so Vinnie decided to go up to his room to read.

After a while he heard Ma come up. Then Clayton climbed the stairs, and the usual night stillness took over. When he was sure everyone must be asleep, Vinnie went out over the roof.

He was partway across the yard when he heard a window being opened behind him. Scared, he dropped flat on the ground and froze, all of him except his heart. Clayton or Ma must have been after some fresh air, he decided, because the night was kind of warm and sticky.

While he waited to find out if he'd been seen, his heart beat so hard and fast it seemed about to break right out of his chest. But no one called to him.

Pa said he was tired.

"I've been down in that water most all day, patching and caulking," he said. "It was real hard work. I dearly wish we could take this boat into some secret little tropical cove and cant her, the way the buccaneers used to do when their ships needed overhauling."

"You don't think she's sound, Pa?" Vinnie almost couldn't bring himself to say such a thing.

"Oh, she's sound enough. When we pump her out, I don't believe much water will come back in after the work I've done. But I'd like to have a real good look at her, all the same."

The air felt strange in the schooner's cabin tonight. Vinnie couldn't decide what was wrong, but it felt heavy, as if the cabin ceiling had dropped down and built up a pressure. Pa said it could mean a change in the weather. "I don't know as much about weather signs as I'd like to," he said. "That's something we'll both have to read up on before too long. If we're going to handle this vessel properly, there's quite a lot we need to know more about, it seems to me."

"Is it the weather making the ship whisper and

creak like this, Pa?"

"I'm sure it is. I'm sure it's natural, too, so don't let it worry you."

"All right." And then, unable to hold it in any longer, Vinnie blurted, "I went to see Liz Maple. Pa, I wish you'd told me!"

"Told you what?" Pa said.

"That she was here."

Pa was quiet for a minute. Then he leaned sideways from the cabin table and opened a cupboard door. It was a green door with colored clouds and big flying birds on it. He took out a bottle of ginger ale and two glasses, poured some of the ginger ale into each glass, and handed one to Vinnie. Then he said, "So she told you, did she?"

Vinnie nodded.

"Well, all right. I guess I should have been the one to tell you, but she asked me not to. We've been friends for years, Liz and I, you know that. But there's nothing more to it than that. I don't cheat on your ma, Vinnie."

"I didn't mean that, Pa. I only meant if we're goin' to be partners—"

"She rowed out here in one of the quahauger boats, same as you do, to see what was going on. Said she couldn't keep on leaving stuff on the cliff for us—lumber and paint and so forth—without knowing what in the world we were up to with it." Pa sipped at his ginger ale. "You like Liz, don't you? I always thought you did."

Again Vinnie nodded.

"She's a fine woman. I don't suppose you know

very much about her, except she owns Maple's grocery."

"No. But I talk to her a lot."

"Liz and I were sweet on each other when we were kids in school," Pa said. "Sort of like you and Mary Raymond, only we were older than you two are. I don't say I was ever in love with her, you understand, but we went around together and I suppose I would have married her if I hadn't met your ma. One thing I know: I always felt good with Liz. I was easy and comfortable, if you know what I mean, even if she wasn't exactly what you'd call a pretty girl. I've never felt quite that much at ease with your ma—and I wish I could. But who knows—maybe one day . . ."

It was too much for Vinnie to take in. Looking around the cabin, he said, "Are we gonna work tonight, Pa?"

"Well, I thought we might, but I don't know what more we can do. That you can help with, I mean."

'We could fix that broken step there. It ought to be fixed, Pa."

"Well, yes, but I'd have to get all my tools out. I'll attend to it later."

Vinnie felt disappointed, kind of. Except for the place saved for Rosanna's picture, there wasn't an inch of space left to paint in the cabin, so he couldn't do any painting. Sure, they could add more stars or birds, things like that, but nothing very big because there just wasn't room enough. Up on deck a lot of work had to be done yet, of course, but they couldn't touch anything there until they got away from the Cape.

"All right, Pa. I better go now."

They went on deck together, Pa saying watch out for the broken step as he always did. Again Vinnie thought the sounds of the schooner were different. He wasn't sure he liked it. There was a straining and twisting going on below, he felt, that might pull things apart. Then again, maybe the difference was that Pa had patched up the hole where he usually tied his skiff, and the skiff was bumping against the new boards now instead of being held fast by the old broken ones.

He hoped none of the quahaugers would take a notion to give the schooner a close look when they rowed their boats out of the cove. The new patch couldn't be seen from the beach, but they'd surely notice it if they came close on the seaward side.

Anyway, the night air felt weird, and when a wave broke against the skiff just as he was reaching for the oars, the spray against his face and hands felt like a warning.

S E V E N T E E N

*T*he next day Clayton went off again to talk to the owner of the yawl that needed rebuilding. Then about eleven o'clock Ma said she had to go look at a neighbor's sewing machine. Clayton had said he would buy it for her to use if she liked it. "You mind Rosanna while I'm gone," she said.

Vinnie put his sister into her high chair and gave her a spoon to play with, then ran to his room for a big piece of paper he'd been saving. It was a poster from a paint company, but Clayton had thrown it away, saying he wouldn't hang up any free advertising for anybody and the least they could have done was put a calendar on it to make it useful.

The poster was white on the back. Vinnie stuck it to the wall in the kitchen with masking tape, so as not to leave any thumbtack marks. Then he got a floor lamp from the parlor and pulled the window shades down and tried for a shadow.

After a while he had it, the lamp throwing the outline of Rosanna's face on the paper when she turned in her chair to watch him. All he had to do was take a soft pencil, the kind used for marking on lumber, and trace around the shadow.

By the time Ma returned, the drawing was hidden in his room and he was back in the kitchen, playing games with Rosanna on the floor.

The weather was raw and cold now. In the afternoon the sky grayed over as if made of smoked glass to block out the sunlight. There was no wind yet, but it was on the way; you could tell. Vinnie almost wished it would come, because the gray sky and cold air seemed even creepier without any kind of proper breeze blowing. When the wind did come, there'd most likely be rain in it. Lots of rain.

In the afternoon he finished what Clayton had told him to do—mostly sweeping up—and went over to the house and played with Rosanna. Suppertime came, and Ma let him feed Rosanna while she fixed something she could keep warm in the oven for Clayton. He must have run into some problems about getting the yawl brought over, she said.

"Aren't you kind of proud you'll be working on a big boat?" she asked him.

Vinnie said, "Sure, Ma," and wondered what she'd think if she knew the kind of job he and Pa were doing on the *Phoenix*. He wished he could tell her. She'd be real proud of the two of them, he was sure. She might even change her mind for sure about Pa.

Clayton got back after nine o'clock and was too tired even to eat the supper Ma had saved for him. He went straight up to bed. Vinnie waited till Ma was in bed, too. Then when the house was dead quiet, he slipped out.

Rowing out to the schooner with the picture of Rosanna rolled up in a piece of canvas, he prayed there wouldn't be a hard rain before he got there. There was no rain. The sea came into the cove in long, smooth swells that were easy to row in.

When he came around the stern of the schooner, though, he found another quahauger skiff tied up alongside Pa's old worthless one. Standing on deck above it, Liz Maple reached down to give him a hand.

"Hi, there, young feller," she said.

He handed her the picture and she pulled him up.

Then they went into the cabin together and Pa was there, putting food away in a cupboard. The cabin table was piled high with all kinds of stuff.

"Think we'll starve, boy?" Pa grinned.

"I guess not." But all of a sudden Vinnie knew he wasn't ready to start out on any voyage. He hadn't thought about it enough. Maybe he never would be ready to leave, unless he could be sure of coming back.

"Thanks to Liz, I guess we won't," Pa said. "Do you know I've done nothing for the past two hours but drag this stuff down the cliff and bring it aboard."

"With my help, I'll thank you to remember," Liz said.

"Without you I couldn't have done it."

"That's better." She put a hand on the side of Vinnie's head and tumbled him against her. Then she held up the roll of canvas and said, "What's this?"

"It's for Pa," Vinnie said, hardly able to wait for Pa to look at what was inside.

She handed the canvas to Pa and he unrolled it. At first he didn't say anything, just held up the picture of Rosanna and studied it. Liz looked at it in silence, too.

It wasn't a good picture, after all, Vinnie guessed when the silence seemed likely to last forever. You could see Pa was disappointed. Pa even looked as if he might cry.

But then Pa placed the picture on the table, putting a box of crackers at one end and a can of corned beef at the other to keep it flat, and said softly, "Vinnie, this is beautiful. It's truly beautiful. Why, it's exactly like having Rosanna here with us, likely to turn her head and start talking to us any minute. How in the world did you manage it, boy?"

Vinnie told him. Then suddenly he blurted out, "Pa, can we go away now? Huh? Can we? Please?"

"You mean tonight? Why the rush?"

What Vinnie wanted to say then was that he couldn't stand the waiting any longer, that he felt he was being torn apart all the time, and the only way to end it was to go. But he couldn't say that. Pa wouldn't understand. What he did say was, "Well, I—I think Clayton knows I've been sneaking out at night, Pa," and he told about hearing the window being opened. Then again he said in a rush of words, "Can we, Pa? Can we leave tonight? I'll go back for my things!"

Pa shook his head. "Liz brought a pump, but I can't get her pumped out that fast. Besides, I don't think you're altogether sure you want to come with me, and when I look at this picture of your sister I can't blame you. *Are* you sure?"

Vinnie couldn't answer.

Pa looked at the picture again and shook his head over it. "To tell the truth, I'm not even sure how *I'd* feel if I had any choice about it," he said.

Liz didn't say anything, and Vinnie was too confused to talk anymore.

But after a moment or two, Vinnie had an idea. "Liz," he said excitedly, "why don't you come with us when we leave?"

"I wish I could, Vinnie."

"Why can't you?"

"Well, I can think of a reason or two, such as I have a store to look after and I don't happen to be married to your father." She laughed a little. "Anyway, don't you suppose this whole idea of a voyage needs to be thought about a bit more? I think it was smart of your father to hide out here on this old boat while deciding what to do next, but I've never said I'm in favor of the rest of it." She turned to look at Pa. "Have I, Joe? Be honest now."

Pa said, "No, you haven't, and that's the truth." Looking at Vinnie, he added, "That's what Liz came aboard for that other time—to convince me I shouldn't take you away from your mother and sister."

"And I still say you shouldn't," Liz said.

"I know you do. But what do *you* say, partner?" Pa looked at Vinnie. "I don't want to walk out on *you*."

Feeling more confused than ever, Vinnie had to think hard before he could answer. Then he said slowly, "Well, it doesn't seem as if Ma wants you back, Pa. She almost said she did once, but she seems to like living at Clayton's now. And she sure doesn't need *me* anymore."

Pa nodded. "That settles it, then, Liz," he said. Liz only looked at him.

When Pa had put everything away, he took Vinnie by the hand and opened another cupboard. The forward locker, he called it. "Here you are, boy," he said, motioning Vinnie to look inside. "The last of our immediate needs."

Before going to work for Clayton Sawtelle, Vinnie

wouldn't have known what he was looking at. He knew now, though. It was a pump. For a boat as big as the *Phoenix* it seemed kind of small, but he didn't feel he knew enough to question that. Pa would have told Liz what size pump to bring, he guessed.

"With that and a whole lot of elbow grease I can pump the water out of this boat and float her," Pa said.

"Wow," Vinnie whispered. Until now he hadn't really pictured the *Phoenix* under sail in the cove here. He'd been able to imagine her in the West Indies or the South Seas, but not here, not sailing out past Dunner Point to begin her journey.

"But like I said, I can't pump her out in one night," Pa went on. "So can you stand Clayton Sawtelle for one more day?"

Clayton was not the problem, Vinnie knew now. The problem was inside himself. But he didn't have to answer, anyway, because Liz did.

"Joe," Liz said, looking troubled, "aren't you rushing into this too fast?"

"We have to go sometime, Liz. And if Sawtelle is watching Vinnie—"

"But the weather. If there's a storm coming—"

"If it gets bad, we'll wait. By the way, we're going to Jamaica. We'll reach there in a couple of weeks, the way I figure it, and can lay up there as long as we want to. That way we can finish fixing up the boat and get the outside of her painted. What color you suppose we ought to paint the outside, Vinnie?"

"I dunno," Vinnie said. "White, maybe, with some gold." With Liz looking at him as if she wanted to cry, it was hard to talk about going away.

"That sounds good to me," Pa said, "and I'm obliged to you, Liz, for bringing more paint. Also for those maps and charts you found for us. Now, what I have in mind is this: We'll drop anchor in some quiet cove down there near a town. Then if we need anything we can go to town and get it, but at the same time we won't be bothered by a lot of curious people hanging around to see what we're up to."

"What'll we use for money, Pa?" Vinnie asked.

"Well, Liz was kind enough to lend me some. I'll be paying her back, of course."

"You make it sound real easy," Liz said. "It won't be, you know."

"No, it won't be easy. I'm aware of that. But we'll manage. Then I have in mind visiting some of those smaller islands at the eastern end of the Caribbean. I have a feeling we can earn a little money there, carrying cargo from one island to another. I figure we might stay in the eastern Caribbean quite a while and build up a nest egg before we move on."

Vinnie was beginning to get excited again. "Then what, Pa?"

"Why, then we can head west again along the north coast of South America, what they used to call the Spanish Main, and go through the canal into the Pacific. Liz, can't you just see the *Phoenix* passing through the Panama Canal with Vinnie and me on deck and people lined up on the banks waving at us?"

"You know how I feel about this, Joe," Liz said.

Vinnie stole a look at her. A change had come over

her while Pa was talking. A kind of sadness. As if she'd been playing a game and suddenly was tired.

Liz stood up. "It's late, Joe. I'd better go."

"It's not all that late," Pa said.

"Yes, it is. I shouldn't have stayed this long with my truck up there on the cliff. You never know who might come along." Turning, she caught hold of Vinnie's hands. "Vinnie, I have to say good-bye, just in case. In this crazy mixed-up world we never know what can happen."

Vinnie tried to answer her but couldn't, and she wrapped her arms around him. He thought he was going to be smothered for sure.

"So long now," she said. "So long, Vinnie. Take good care of yourself."

"Sure, Liz."

"And Vinnie . . ."

"Yeah?"

"Remember what I told you. If things don't work out the way you hope, it won't be the end of the world."

"Sure, Liz."

She let him go then, and Pa said, "Suppose you go on deck for a minute, Vinnie, while I have a word with Liz in private. Or maybe you're ready to go ashore now."

"I can go ashore, Pa."

Going on deck with Vinnie, Pa used the broken step without thinking and it bent under him, throwing him off balance. He would have fallen if Vinnie hadn't grabbed him.

"Now, look at that," he said. "I keep meaning to fix

it, and it slips my mind every time. I'll do it tonight, right after Liz goes."

On deck he laid a hand on Vinnie's shoulder. "Sometime tomorrow, boy, if you can do it without your ma or Clayton being suspicious, you'd better get your things together," he said. "You'll need whatever clothes you've got, I should think, hot and cold weather both, and—well, I guess you've done some thinking about it already."

Vinnie nodded.

"Come aboard as early tomorrow night as you can. I'll try to have her pumped out, and the sail on, and everything ready for us to go."

"Sure, Pa."

"All right, then. Down you go."

Vinnie dropped into his skiff and rowed ashore. When the boat was put away properly, so its owner wouldn't know it had been borrowed, he stood there and looked at it, realizing it would be a problem tomorrow night. After rowing out to the schooner in it, how would he get it back here if he left with Pa? But Pa must have thought of that and would know what to do.

Walking back along the beach, he noticed how clammy the night air was. There was a breeze now, too, coming in short, quick gusts with a sound like a kettle whistling on a stove.

All the way to where he climbed the bluff he saw only one creature moving. That was a hurt crab that crawled only a few feet out of the water and then was caught by a wave and washed back again.

EIGHTEEN

*H*e thought the next day would never end. It would be his last day at Clayton Sawtelle's; he knew that. Pa needed him.

In the morning, while feeding Rosanna her breakfast, he kept wondering if he would ever get used to not having her around, laughing at him and saying his name. Thinking about it made him feel all torn up inside again.

And Ma. When he thought of not seeing Ma again, he almost couldn't stand it.

Ma, Rosanna, Liz—it was going to be sad, not being with any of them again. Steve Dennis, too. He probably would never see Steve again. And what about Mary Raymond? True, he'd hardly talked to her lately, but not to be with her ever again . . .

Right after breakfast Clayton decided to do some work in the boat shed, even though it was Saturday. "We'd better make sure we can accommodate that yawl when she's delivered," he said. "Come on, Vinnie. I can use you."

The old man wanted all sorts of things moved around in the shed, including the two Camp Wildeway skiffs. He was annoyed that the skiffs were still there. "That man Perkins must think we have unlimited storage space," he grumbled. "If he thinks at all, which I doubt."

"You mean he's still supposed to come for them?" Vinnie said.

"Of course."

Vinnie hadn't thought about the boats and the camp director in quite a while. There'd been too much else on his mind. Going away with Pa would take care of that problem, he realized with a feeling of relief. He wouldn't have to worry anymore about facing Mr. Perkins.

At lunch Clayton was tired, and nobody said much until Ma got a conversation started by asking about the weather. Clayton didn't like the looks of it. "I wouldn't want to be out there right now on anything but a real stout ship," he said. "To be truthful, I wouldn't want to be out there at all."

Afterward Vinnie returned to the shed with Clayton, and they moved more things around. Then about three o'clock a truck rattled into the yard. Vinnie looked out a window to see whose it was.

It was the Camp Wildeway pickup, with Ev Hutton driving and Steve Dennis sitting beside him. And next to Steve sat the camp director, Mr. Perkins.

Numb with fright, Vinnie stood glued to the shed floor while Perkins got out and came toward the door. There was no way he could escape. If he ran out, he would run right into the man. He could only stand there and wait, remembering what Steve Dennis had told him—that Perkins was a man who never forgot anyone who made him look bad.

The camp director hadn't changed any, Vinnie

saw. He was still tall and skinny with a streak of red hair on his lip. He even wore the same kind of clothes he had worn when he caught Vinnie: tight khaki pants tucked into leather boots and a khaki shirt. He came into the shed now and Clayton, with a puzzled glance at Vinnie, turned to greet him.

Then Perkins saw Vinnie. He stopped dead in his tracks and his face turned a funny pink. His hand shot out, pointing. "You!" he yelled. "Come here!"

Taking a backward step instead, Vinnie flattened himself against a wall.

"What in the world's the matter?" Clayton said, peering from one to the other.

"This boy!" the camp director sputtered. "Who is he?"

"Name's Vincent Blake. What's he done that you're so upset about?"

"He's a thief! I've been looking for him for weeks!"

Clayton's face took on a scowl that showed he wasn't pleased. But whether he was displeased with Vinnie or with Perkins, Vinnie couldn't tell. Staring at Vinnie, he said, "What have you got to say about this, boy?"

Vinnie walked toward them, wondering if he could get past them to the door and make a run for it. They wouldn't catch him if he got outside the shed. He could make for the cove and they wouldn't even know where he'd gone.

But he didn't want to go to Pa that way. Pa had problems enough.

"You say this boy's a thief?" This time Clayton was

scowling at the camp man. "Just what did he steal from you, Mr. Perkins?"

"I caught him trying to steal food from the camp kitchen!"

"Is that right, Vinnie?"

"Yes, sir."

"You see?" Perkins shouted. "He admits it!"

"I was hungry," Vinnie said, surprised at how easy it was, after all, not to be scared. Turning from Clayton, he stood as straight as he knew how to and fixed his gaze on Perkins. "My ma was hungry, too, and my sister. And I never got the food—you took it away from me before you locked me in your office—so I don't know what you're so sore about. I never even got to take home the blackberries I worked all day for. You took those away from me, too, along with the pail. You told one of your kids to throw the pail and all into your garbage pit."

Perkins opened his mouth to say something but didn't say it because Clayton had taken a step toward him and was glaring at him. Perkins looked as if Vinnie had slapped him hard across the face, and Clayton might do it again.

"Is this true, what the boy is saying, Mr. Perkins?" Clayton's cold blue eyes were colder than Vinnie had ever seen them.

"Yes, it is," said a voice from behind him. "Every word of it, Mr. Sawtelle."

Vinnie and Clayton and Perkins all looked toward the door, and there stood Steve Dennis, with his hands clamped on his hips and his head thrust forward. "That's exactly what Mr. Perkins did, sir.

When he caught Vinnie in the kitchen, he didn't even talk to him to find out why he was taking that food. He just marched him over to the camp office and locked him up."

Still with his hands on his hips, Steve turned to look at Perkins. "And, yes, Mr. Perkins, I was the one who let Vinnie out of the office that day," he said. "I wouldn't tell you before, even when you caught me talking to him at the old tree and threatened to send me home, but I'm telling you now. And for your information, I'm going home tomorrow. I phoned my folks and they're coming for me, and my dad will have a few things to say to you."

The camp director's face was gray as putty.

"What really did it," Steve went on, "was when you stole Vin's blackberries and had them thrown away. You didn't even want them. You just wanted to show the kids how tough you were."

"What's your name, son?" Clayton said.

"Steve Dennis, sir."

"I just want to say I'm glad to know you." Then Clayton turned to Perkins. "As for you, sir," he said in a voice that sounded like a file rubbing rust off a piece of metal, "I'll thank you to hand me a check for your two boats, after which my friend Vinnie and I will load them onto your pickup and you can take them out of here. And I hope never to see your face or hear your voice again."

Perkins was not a brave man. He returned the older man's stare for only a few seconds in silence. Then he turned and walked over to a bench and took out a checkbook. By that time Ev Hutton had come in from the doorway where Vinnie had seen him standing for quite some time. Ev was smiling with obvious pleasure.

Still without a word, the camp director handed a check to Clayton. Then Clayton and Vinnie, with a little help from Ev and Steve Dennis, got the boats onto the truck.

Afterward, Steve Dennis handed Vinnie a piece of paper. "This is where I live and my phone number," he said. "I guess I won't be seeing you again this summer. I hope we can be friends, though."

"Me, too!" Vinnie said. "Thanks for talking to Perkins the way you did. I don't think I could have handled it by myself."

"Sure you could." Steve grinned.

"I'm surprised he brought you today."

"He had to. You remember that medal for leadership?"

"Yeah."

"It isn't just a medal. It gets you certain privileges. When Ev told me they were coming for the boats, I said I was coming, too, and there was no way Perkins could stop me without making trouble for himself. I wasn't gonna let him come without me. No way!" Steve grinned again. "Well, hey, Ev's calling me. So long now."

"So long," Vinnie said.

The pickup rolled out of the yard with Steve and Ev waving and Perkins looking grim. Then Clayton came into the boat shed.

"You can get on with your work now, boy," Clayton said. "But in case you've got any wrong ideas

about what just happened, I want you to know I
don't hold with stealing, even when I admire your
spunk. You understand?"

"Yes, sir," Vinnie said. But when he smiled, Clayton kind of smiled back.

"It'll be my pleasure to tell Wesley about this when
he comes home," the old man added.

N I N E T E E N

At supper Vinnie fed Rosanna, thinking it
was the last time he'd be sitting with her
for a while, teasing her into grabbing at his free
hand while he spooned food into her. But he was
glad when Clayton went to bed right after eating,
saying he'd had three or four hard days in a row and
needed more than his usual amount of rest.

To be with Ma as long as he could, Vinnie helped
with the dishes. She washed and he dried, and he
took so long doing it that she said once, "My goodness, you don't have to polish the forget-me-nots off
them!" It was the first time he'd been aware the little
blue flowers on Clayton's dishes were forget-me-
nots.

"Well," he said at last, "g'night, Ma."

"You're going to bed this early?"

"I guess I'm kind of tired, too."

"My goodness," she said. "It looks like a lonely
evening ahead for me, with Clayton and you both
gone to bed. Although I don't usually see much of

you in the evenings anymore, do I? Well, good-night."

He would have kissed her if he could have done it without her wondering—even asking, maybe—what had gotten into him. He had to be content to look at her, so he would be sure to remember how pretty she was with her soft, dark hair and all. Even if he only went to the islands with Pa and then came back here, he would feel as if a part of his life had come to an end.

"Ma . . ."

"Yes, Vinnie?"

"I—I just—I love you, Ma."

She drew him up close to her, putting her face against his. "Vinnie, I know you do," she said in a soft voice. "And I love you, too. Don't you ever forget it."

When she let him go, he ran to his room and closed the door.

Bring all the clothes you have, Pa had said. Warm weather and cold weather both, because they would be going to both kinds of places. He wouldn't need cold weather clothes if he came straight back from the islands, though.

He had an empty cardboard box in the closet, saved from the boat shed. A few days ago Ma had asked what he wanted it for, and he'd said it was just too good to throw away. "You never know when you'll need a nice clean box, Ma," he'd said.

He got the box out and started to put things into it, trying not to make any sounds that might wake Clayton or cause Ma to wonder what he was up to.

He put in a pair of pants, a shirt, underwear, the sweater Ma had given him for his birthday, his extra pair of shoes, his jacket. . . . The box was full when he finished. It wasn't too heavy for him to handle, though. He could manage it by sliding it down the roof after him. Only if it got past him somehow and dropped off would it make too much noise.

When he had packed everything that he thought he might need, he tied the box and put it far back in the closet and shut the door on it. Then he undressed and got into bed and put his light out. He had to be in bed if Ma walked in for some reason. Not that she often did, but she might.

Lying in the dark, he listened to the sound of the wind. All day, off and on, he'd been hearing it. At the boat shed it had made the windows thump and rattle, and once caused a rippling sound among the roof shingles as if a squirrel had been chasing around up there. At supper, with no one talking much, he'd heard it howling and whistling around the house at times. Now it sang in the tall pines between his bedroom and the road.

It was steadier now, too, not so gusty as earlier in the day. If it got any stronger, he might have a hard time rowing out to the schooner. Never mind, he told himself; he'd get there. And Pa would have the *Phoenix* pumped out, or almost pumped out, and they would hoist the sail and take her out of the cove. With a wind like this they could be miles away from the Cape by daylight. No one would know where to look for them. Only Liz knew where they were going.

Maybe Liz would explain things to Ma. Vinnie hoped she would.

Just then he heard Ma's footsteps on the stairs. She paused at the top and he thought for a second she might suspect something. But she must have stopped to look along the hall and see if there was a light under his door. He was not supposed to go to sleep with his light on. In the old house where they'd used oil lamps it wasn't so bad, but here Clayton had to pay an electric bill. He heard her door click shut and looked at his clock, holding it close to his eyes so he could see the time.

Come as early as you can, Pa had said. He would give Ma half an hour. She'd be asleep by then.

Did he want to go? No, he didn't. It was clear in his mind now: He didn't. But he had to. There was no way around it.

Fifteen minutes had gone by.

Vinnie got up and dressed in the dark, then sat on the bed to wait again. It seemed like forever, but at last the waiting time ended and he inched his door open to look along the hall.

Ma's door was dark. So was Clayton's. Closing his own again without making any noise, he lifted the box from the closet and carried it to the window. He slid the sash up so slowly it didn't make a sound.

When he had squirmed through the opening, he turned and reached back into the room, lifted the box off the floor, and pulled it through. It was tricky, guiding the box down after him while he eased himself down the kitchen roof and dropped to the woodshed below, but he managed it. Easing himself from the woodshed to the yard, he slid the box down into his arms.

The wind was stronger. When he got away from the house, it came whistling along the edge of the bluff and all but tore the box out of his grasp. The gusts brought tears to his eyes as he crossed the yard.

Then at the edge of the yard he remembered the blankets, and stopped.

Now that he was clear of the house, out of danger, he didn't want to go back. His heart had only just begun to slow down. But he didn't want the two of them to be shivering from the cold every night on board the *Phoenix*, either. He just had to have those blankets.

Lowering the box into tall grass at the yard's edge, he turned to look back. There were no lights on in the house.

He hurried back, minding the loss of time more than anything else. The wind was real strong now. He could hear the sea pounding at the base of the bluff, like thunder in a storm coming closer. It took only a minute to scramble back up to his window, though, and pull one blanket off his bed and another out of the closet. They were only light-weight blankets this time of year, thank the Lord. Really heavy ones would have been too much for him.

With the blankets under one arm, not even folded right, he slid down to the yard again, landing in a heap when the weight of his burden pulled him off balance. Jumping up, he started to run.

There in front of him, like a scraggly old tree bent by the wind, stood Clayton Sawtelle.

Vinnie stopped dead in his tracks and felt his whole body begin to shake.

"You going somewhere?" the old man said. His voice was not a shout, but it was loud enough to bounce off the back wall of the house before a gust of wind carried it away.

Vinnie took a step backward.

"Don't run," Clayton said. "You can't get out of this by running, boy. It's your father you've been sneaking out to see nights, isn't it?"

Vinnie couldn't think of anything to say. He stopped shaking, though, and stood tall.

"Your father," Clayton said again, "who ought to be in jail finishing his sentence."

Vinnie found his voice at last. "I don't have to tell you nothin'!"

"Anything," Clayton corrected. "But you do. Long as you and your ma and Rosanna are living in my house, I'm responsible for you, sort of. Now, suppose you tell me where your father is, and what you hoped to do with those blankets."

Even with the wind doing its noisy best to bowl him over, Vinnie stood his ground. "You owe me enough to pay for the blankets, Mr. Sawtelle."

"Do I? Well, perhaps I do, so we won't make an issue of that. But they're for your father, aren't they? Because he needs them to keep him warm at night. So I'm puzzled as to where he can be hiding out, and I think you'd better tell me."

"No."

"No?"

"That's what he said, Clayton." This new voice came from the kitchen doorway. "He said 'no,' and he's right. This isn't your affair, much as we appreciate your concern."

Startled, Vinnie swung around to look at the doorway and saw Ma standing there. There was no light in the kitchen behind her, so he wouldn't have seen her if she hadn't been wearing a white nightgown. It made her look like a ghost, or what he thought a ghost ought to look like, and even more so as she sort of glided toward them.

"You be quiet now, Vinnie, and let me do the talking for a minute," she said, reaching out to touch him on the arm. Then, facing Clayton, she said in a real calm voice, "Yes, Clayton, Vinnie is right. This is a family matter and something for my son and me to settle. It's none of your business."

"You're talking about a man who escaped from jail," Clayton said, sounding angry now.

"But not about a dangerous criminal," Ma said, "and I'm sure a man of your worldly knowledge must appreciate the difference. I didn't know Joe was in hiding around here. I had no idea. But if he is, and if Vinnie has been helping him, I can't see anything so wrong in it. Certainly nothing that gives you the right to interfere."

Clayton stared at her in silence, working his jaws as if he were chewing on a tough piece of meat.

"If this is costing us our jobs here, so be it," Ma said. "I've been glad of the work, and I'm grateful

167

for the way you stood up for Vinnie against that Mr. Perkins today, believe me. But this business with Joe Blake is something for Vinnie and me to settle. Not you."

"You mean you're going to take Joe back?" Clayton said.

"I've been thinking about it."

"He'd have to finish his sentence first."

"If he gives himself up to do that, it won't be for long. Only a few months, at most."

"And you'd be going back to your old house?"

"Of course."

"Oh, Lord," Clayton said. "Just when I thought I'd got that problem solved."

"You've got a bigger problem solved, Clayton." All at once Ma's voice was no longer firm but soft and gentle. "If Wesley's coming back, it must mean you and he have reached an understanding. The two of you won't have any trouble finding another house-keeper."

The way they were talking, Vinnie could see it might last a long time. "Ma," he said, "can I go?"

"Can you go where?" Ma said.

"To Pa. Maybe I can bring him back!"

Ma looked at how the wind was tearing at the pine trees. "How can you go anywhere in this weather?"

"It isn't far."

"Well . . ."

That was all Vinnie needed. Dropping the blankets, he turned and ran at full speed into the gusty dark, not even stopping at the end of the yard to pick up his box of belongings.

Ma had said she would take Pa back. He had to get to Pa and tell him!

T W E N T Y

The dark didn't trouble him. He knew the way to the schooner now as well as he knew the way from Clayton's kitchen to the boat shed. But that wind was a thing to be reckoned with.

It came from behind him, sweeping down past the house, tearing through the high grass at the bluff's edge. It had rain in it or sea spray, maybe some of both, that wet and chilled his clothes while the gusts held them close against him. There was real danger, too. If he lost control sliding down the cliff with a mass of wet sand pouring down after him, he could be in big trouble.

The cove beach was all noise, with waves crashing and white water pouring almost up to the line of quahauger boats. Only after he'd stood there for a minute, with the water hissing around his ankles, was he able to make out the schooner.

Had Pa pumped her out? She didn't seem to be riding any higher than before, but with the sea heaving like that you couldn't tell for sure.

Soaked to the skin now, he struggled to turn a skiff over. The cold made him shiver, but the noise was the worst thing. The noise was plain scary. With waves crashing here where he had to launch the boat, and even louder explosions down the beach where the rocks were, he had a hard time even thinking straight.

But he got the boat into the water. He got it pushed out through the first line of breakers without letting it be swamped. He was able to scramble into it and snatch up the oars.

For a time it seemed he made more progress up and down than forward. Wave after wave lifted the boat's bow high up in the screaming dark, then let it plunge back down again. Time and again he had to stop rowing and brace himself. Once an oar slipped from his grasp and almost got away from him.

But at last, just when he thought he wasn't big enough or strong enough to win out, the shattering waves that could swamp a boat fell behind him. The skiff inched ahead through heaving swells instead. Turning his head, he saw he was going to make it to the schooner after all, and knew Pa would be proud of him.

The schooner should be higher in the water, though, shouldn't she? She should be if Pa had pumped her out, he thought.

He brought the skiff up against the *Phoenix*, shipping his oars barely in time to keep one of them from being snapped off like a match against the boat's side. Pa was there on deck, reaching down and yelling at him to pass up the painter. With the sea heaving him up and down he crawled forward and got the rope and stood up with it, and Pa grabbed it. Then Pa pulled him up on deck and led him to the cabin.

"I never thought you'd try to come in weather like this," Pa said. Because of the storm noise he had to yell it.

Things were better in the cabin, with the door shut. The ship creaked and groaned without rest, and every little while had a fit of trembling, as if she were alive and scared. But here the louder sounds of sea and wind were muffled. Dropping onto his bed under the pine board with his name carved on it, Vinnie looked around at all the handsome painting Pa had done.

"Pa, I got something to tell you."

"Wait," Pa said. "I've something to tell you first, boy." He sat on the opposite bed and leaned forward with his hands on his knees, while the ship jerked and jumped like a living thing and the light from the lantern danced all over the walls.

"But, I—"

"Wait," Pa said again. "First, let me tell you I been pumping all day long and I do believe I got most of the water out. She may not seem to be riding any higher because she's caught in the sand and won't actually float until she breaks loose. But, Vinnie, listen. Listen to me now. I have to tell you something that's pretty hard for me to say, especially when we seem so close to being ready."

Something was wrong, Vinnie saw. He looked at Pa's face in the dancing light of the lantern and there was no joy in it, only sadness. Not a little sadness, either, but a whole world of it, deep and terrible. He couldn't recall a time when Pa had ever looked like that before, not even when everything had gone wrong for him at home. Pa had even laughed at trouble sometimes.

"What is it, Pa?" he asked, feeling cold with fright.

"We can't sail this boat out of here," Pa said. "That's what I have to tell you, son. We can't do it. I thought we might be able to, but we can't."

"What, Pa?"

"First, I couldn't handle any boat this big even if we sailed her out of here," Pa said, looking down at the floor now. "I don't know any navigation. I'm not even sure I could put a sail on her so's it would stay on. It was only an idea I had."

Vinnie sat and stared at him, feeling numb. Hearing such a statement was one thing; believing it was another. He couldn't let himself believe it.

"Pa, you fixed her up. She's beautiful!"

Pa shook his head. "You don't fix up a boat like this just by nailing some boards over the holes in her and painting her cabin."

"But you said you pumped her out. If you could do that—"

"Uh-uh." Pa sat there with that sad look on his face. "No, boy, we can't go anywhere. I knew it all along, I guess. Liz did, too. I only worked on the boat to help me think about what I ought to do with the rest of my life. Because I hadn't decided that, Vinnie. I love Ma and Rosanna. I knew I couldn't run off and leave them, even if your ma didn't want me back. I couldn't take you away, either, because I love you, boy. I knew I had a weakness for dreaming."

"There's nothin' wrong with dreamin', Pa!"

"No, there isn't. As I told your ma once, if no-body'd ever done any of it since the world began, we'd still be living in caves and wearing the skins of animals to keep us warm. But a man ought to keep his dreams under control, and sometimes I don't do that."

"Pa . . ."

There were tears in Pa's eyes when he raised his head to look at Vinnie and said, "What, lad?"

"Ma wants you to come back."

"What?"

"She wants you, Pa. It's what I been trying to tell you."

Pa took in a big breath and his whole face changed. "She told you that?"

"She told Clayton. If you finish up your time in jail and come back to us, we can move back to the old house, she said."

"Vinnie, you're not just saying this to make me feel good about the boat, are you?"

"No, Pa. It's the truth!"

Pa stood up and took in another big breath. It made him seem taller. "Well!" he said, and the word came out like a soft explosion. "Where's your ma now? At Sawtelle's?"

"Yes, Pa."

"Then let's get out of here and go talk to her! I *will* finish up my time in jail. I'll call the police this very night so I can get started on it. Come on, boy!"

He stretched out a hand to help Vinnie off the bed, and Vinnie all but cried for joy as he reached for it. Then all at once Vinnie became aware that the bed was shaking.

"Pa!" He grabbed at Pa's hand and jumped up.

More than the bed was moving, he saw then. The whole cabin was starting to heave. The floor came up like a wave, and Pa pitched forward onto his knees. The lantern began a wild swinging back and forth, thumping the wall. Things on the floor slid from one end of the cabin to the other or fetched up against the legs of the table.

Pa recovered and scrambled to his feet, wild-eyed. "Oh, my Lord!" he yelled. "She's torn loose! She's afloat!"

The cabin floor rose up then in a series of lurchings, with a sound underneath it of water rushing toward the ship's bow. All at once the *Phoenix* heeled far over and Vinnie found himself sprawled on one of the painted walls, with Pa grabbing at him.

"She'll turn over or be blown out to sea!" Pa shouted. "We got to get off her, Vinnie!"

There was another wild heave, and the cabin was right side up again with Vinnie in a heap on the floor. Pa grabbed him and pulled him toward the stairs. "Hurry!" Pa yelled. "We don't have much time!"

The schooner was free of the sand's grip and moving now; you could tell. The feel of her was different, even with all the heaving. She was alive and racing, the way Vinnie had pictured her under clouds of white canvas among the islands of the West Indies or the South Seas.

But she was racing to her death, he knew. There was a terrible sound of water sloshing around inside her. Either she would fetch up on those big rocks at the far side of the cove, near the quahaugers' houses, or she would slip through to the open sea and go under. She couldn't have more than a few minutes of life left in her.

"Come on!" Pa yelled, dragging him up the stairs. "We can get ashore in your skiff!"

Then suddenly there was a sharp, crackling sound as a board broke, and Pa was down on one knee. That old broken step had snapped under him and let his leg through.

"Oh, Lord," Pa said. "Here. Give me a hand."

With Vinnie tugging at him he tried to draw the leg back up, but it wouldn't come. The splintery jaws of the board only tightened more, holding him as if he were caught in a vise.

The ship heeled far over again and Pa let out a groan. It was not only a groan of pain; it was full of hopelessness, too. "You told me," he said while Vinnie frantically pulled at him. "Time and again you told me to fix it. Pull, boy, pull!"

Vinnie got hold of the trapped leg just above the knee and tugged with all his might, but the leg wouldn't budge. He looked at Pa's pain-twisted face and saw that the tugging was about killing him. Pulling wouldn't be enough, anyway.

The schooner swayed far over again, and a torrent of dark water poured down the steps into the cabin. It almost swept Vinnie off his feet. He hung onto Pa, though, and when it passed he was still there, doing his best. On his knees now, he tried with all his strength to spread the broken board-ends apart so Pa could draw his leg out. He was doing that when the next wall of water hit them.

This time Vinnie had to throw his arms around Pa's neck to keep from being slammed across the cabin, and Pa could see that the next rush of water would be the end. "Vinnie," Pa moaned, "get out of here while you can. Go on! Clear out!"

"No, Pa."

"We'll both drown if you don't, son! Go on, I tell you! Save yourself! Ma and Rosanna need you!"

"No," Vinnie said, and let go of Pa and scrambled on hands and knees to the locker where the tools Liz had brought were stored. He remembered seeing a crowbar there that might do the job if he could handle it.

The schooner lurched and tossed him against the locker door, all but knocking him senseless. Water poured over him like a river, rolling him back across the floor. He swallowed enough to fill his mouth with salt, and saw a rainbow of colored lights from the shock as he struggled up on hands and knees and tried again. This time he made it to the locker and got the door open.

When he got back to Pa, dragging the heavy metal bar after him, Pa was barely able to talk. In such a low voice that Vinnie scarcely heard him, he said again, "Save yourself, Vinnie, please! They need you!" Then his eyes closed and Vinnie guessed he'd passed out from the pain.

On his knees, Vinnie got the bar into position under one end of the broken step while the *Phoenix* all but turned over again and yet another wall of water crashed into him. This time the crowbar saved him because it was wedged in place and he had a grip on it. The water passed and he put his whole weight on the bar, and the board snapped.

"Pa, you're free! Hang onto me, Pa!"

There must have been a breath of awareness left in Pa, after all. One hand reached out to clutch feebly at Vinnie's shirt. The other tried to grab something, too, but missed and slid over Vinnie's face like wet seaweed. Then the moment fled and Pa went limp again.

But he was free. Dropping the crowbar, Vinnie got hold of him under the arms and struggled to haul him up the cabin steps that had caused all the trouble. Step by step he succeeded, even though the sea was doing its best to turn the schooner over and masses of water were pouring down on him.

Near the end, he had Pa up on deck and Pa was conscious again, and they were hanging onto each other for dear life as a huge wave flipped the schooner on her side. With that they were swept off the deck together and the wild sea swallowed them.

For a while after that all Vinnie knew was a dark, cold sea full of sound and fury that swept him through or past the rocks and then, amid explosions of surf, tossed him up on the beach. There he lay, bruised and shivering, sick at heart, certain Pa was dead.

But when he felt strong enough to get up and go

look, he found Pa only twenty yards or so away, dragging one leg behind him as he crawled over the sand.

"Pa!"

Pa stopped crawling and struggled to sit up. "Vinnie, is that you?"

"Yes, Pa! Yes!"

"I was looking for you." Pa held out his arms. "Thank God for a miracle. Thank God you're alive."

Vinnie sank down beside him. "Pa, are you hurt?"

"That broken step didn't do me any good, boy. My leg's broken, too, I think. What you might do . . ." Pa turned his head to look along the beach. "Did I hear someone calling?"

Vinnie had heard something, too. In the dark he couldn't see much except the white foam of crashing waves, and for a minute he didn't hear anything except the thunder of those waves among the rocks. Then, yes, he heard a voice calling his name. And down the beach a way he saw the beam of a flashlight swinging back and forth.

Two people—at least, he thought he saw two— were walking along the beach toward him. Could they be quahaugers? No quahauger would be out at night in weather like this. There were only two people on earth who might be looking for him here at this time!

"Ma!" he yelled, jumping up and waving his arms. "Ma! Over here!"

The two shapes stopped, and the flashlight beam searched for him.

"Vinnie," Pa said, reaching up to him. "Do you mean your ma's coming?"

"Yes, Pa! And someone else. It has to be Clayton! They must have figured out where I was goin'!"

"Vinnie," Pa said, "bend down so I can talk without yelling."

Vinnie dropped to one knee and leaned over him.

"Listen," Pa said. "If I should pass out again before they get here, you be sure to tell them I plan on calling the police. And tell them I'd appreciate their help in getting this broken leg looked after. Will you do that, son?"

"You bet!" Vinnie said, then jumped up again and ran toward the approaching figures. Both of them were bundled up in rain gear, he saw now, but yes, they were Ma and Clayton, and when they saw him running toward them they broke into a run, too.

The *Phoenix* was gone, Vinnie discovered when he left Clayton Sawtelle's house and went down to the cove the next morning. Being driven onto the rocks that way, she must have broken up into kindling wood. He walked along the water's edge and saw all kinds of things washed ashore from her—spars and planks, lengths of rope, even one of the cupboard doors Pa had painted with so much love.

The storm had passed. The sun was out now and the sea was almost back to normal. Suddenly he stopped.

In front of him, half buried in the sand at the water's edge, were two pieces of wood. One had the schooner's name on it—*Phoenix*—and the other was the pine board on which Pa had carved *his* name. He pulled them out of the sand and wiped them off.

They were things to keep, both of them.

Forever.